000 個最常考的單字

NEW TOEIC

隨書附贈 MP3

U0119824

新多益黃金單字

滿分狀元的訣竅，
只背會考的單字！

NEW TOEIC
六度滿分狀元 **文之勤** 著

10 大職場情境主題
以最常見的商業活動情境為主軸，從社交會面到企業營運，分門別類精選最實用的高出題率單字。

2000 個搶分延伸單字
每個單字都附有可同時學習的延伸字，一次學會所有相關單字群組，系統性的快速增加單字量。

10 回單字測驗+精闢解析
單字測驗模擬新多益實際出題方式及測驗難度，輔以精闢解析，徹底提升新多益單字深度與廣度。

100 分鐘黃金單字學習 MP3
單字例句全部收錄，外籍老師清晰發音，上班途中、會議空檔或睡前片刻，
隨時隨地學習記憶，聽力測驗必得高分。

目錄　**Table of Contents**

前言 Preface

單字量的重要性

英文「單字量」(vocabulary) 是在英語學習「聽／說／讀／寫」過程中相當重要的基礎。若認識的單字很侷限，或雖然認識某個單字，卻只知道一種意思，換個用法就不會了等情況，難免聽老外說話時可能會錯意，閱讀文章時一直被卡住，更不用提要開口講或書寫文章時，因為可運用的單字量少，而產生詞不達意的窘境。

背單字的優先順序

那麼，單字量的多寡對英語學習會產生如此大的影響，同學們應如何來拓展自己的單字量呢？筆者最常聽到同學們提及的問題，就是應該抱著整本英文字典來背呢？還是一定要背難的單字才算有增加到單字量呢？事實上，只要大約認識 6,000 ~ 8,000 個重要單字，就足以應付日常生活的溝通。若辦公環境中需要開會、談判或書寫報告，那麼最好至少有 9,000 ~ 10,000 個單字為基礎，比較可以運用發揮，TOEIC 考試的單字量也在此範圍內。 既然如此，同學們所應該做的，就是將精力先放在

認識並熟悉日常溝通時真正會用到的單字上。而且，並不是知道怎麼拼、怎麼唸，學會單一意思就足夠，而是要連帶地對單字的用法、詞性、其他意思、同義字等都加以瞭解，以利往後在不同情境下的使用。

TOEIC 單字的焦點

因此，本書提供的是日常應用以及 TOEIC 考試，必備的最實用 1,000 單字。每個單字除了包括中文意思、音標唸法、詞性、例句之外，還增加了 2~3 個延伸字，在認識某一個單字的同時，更拓展學習範圍，達到多出 2~3 倍的單字量。本書另一特點是單字並非單純由 A-Z 來排列，而是依照日常辦公環境常見的「情境」來分類，包括社交、面談、會議等主題情境。讓同學們可以更瞭解單字在某個情境之下的使用方式。

最後，期望同學們可以把 TOEIC 單字當成一個學習的切入點，除了考試拿到高分，更能打穩日後在職場上的具體應用基礎。

文之勤

2014 年 3 月

使用說明

本書以新多益常見的十大主題為軸心，精心歸納出 1000 個新多益必考單字，為出題頻率最高、最能辨別考生程度的單字。輔以清楚、易讀的呈現方式，讓考生能系統性地學習吸收，掌握新多益高分的先機。本書學習規劃如下：

Step 1 學習單字，培養實力

社交
會面

MP3
1

○ accompany

[ə`kʌmpənɪ]

(v.) 陪同，伴隨

Would you like us to **accompany** you on your way back home?

你是否希望我們陪你一起回家？

延伸字 escort, go out with, follow

○ accountability

[ə͵kaʊntə`bɪlətɪ]

(n.) 負責任，
有義務

Since we're discussing the **accountability** here, I think you are also accountable.

既然我們正在討論責任歸屬，我認為你也需要負責任。

延伸字 responsibility, liability

○ acknowledgment

[ək`nɑlɪdʒmənt]

(n.) 確認，認可，
收到通知

I am still waiting for the **acknowledgment** from the top.

我仍然在等待高層的確認。

延伸字 recognition, appreciation, confirmation

MP3 1 ❶

▸ **accompany**
[ə`kʌmpənɪ]
(v.) 陪同，伴隨 ❷

Would you like us to **accompany** you on your way back home?
你是否希望我們陪你一起回家？❹
延伸字 escort, go out with, follow ❸

❶ 表示本頁單字所在音軌。MP3 中唸讀單字及例句各一遍，可熟悉單字正確的發音，對於聽力測驗及日常表達皆有幫助。

❷ 標示單字的詞性與中文解釋。瞭解單字的詞性可避免文法上的誤用，中文解釋則以新多益測驗中最常見的用法為主。

❸ 列舉延伸字。在學習單字的同時，一併學習衍生的相關字，可以有效增加字彙量，並有助於閱讀測驗部分的解題。

❹ 例句中英文對照。以新多益測驗常見的語句為主，並提供適切且自然的中文解釋，以提升聽力及閱讀的流暢度。

Step 2 實力測驗，自我檢視

Test 1

Q1. My name is Lily Chen. I have an _____ with Ms. Anderson at 3.
(A) affirmation
(B) appointment
(C) excellence
(D) application

Q2. It's a (n) _____ to meet you, Mr. Steve.
(A) strategy
(B) opportunity
(C) fortune
(D) pleasure

Q3. Our company has its _____ in Singapore.
(A) rooms
(B) wrinkles
(C) beverage
(D) headquarters

Q4. Our _____ product manager will speak at this conference, as the manager is on business travel.
(A) deputy
(B) depressed
(C) domestic
(D) disnatured

020　新多益黃金單字

Step 3 檢討答案，加深記憶

Test 1

Q1. My name is Lily Chen. I have an _____ with Ms. Anderson at 3.

我是陳莉莉。我三點跟 Anderson 小姐有約。

(A) affirmation 證實

(B) appointment 約會

(C) excellence 完美

(D) application 應用

Q2. It's a _____ to meet you, Mr. Steve.

很榮幸認識您，Steve 先生。

(A) strategy 策略

(B) opportunity 機會

(C) fortune 運氣

(D) pleasure 榮幸

Q3. Our company has its _____ in Singapore.

我們公司總部設在新加坡。

(A) rooms 房間

(B) wrinkles 皺紋

(C) beverage 飲料

(D) headquarters 總部

使用
說明

　　「單字實力測驗」共有十回，每回皆有 20 題克漏字考題，模擬新多益實際出題方式及測驗難度，作答完畢後，搭配中文詳解檢討答案，進一步加深自己的理解程度與單字實力。各回答對題數所代表意義如下：

17 題以上：對於大部分新多益必考單字及其用法已有充分瞭解。

13 ~ 16 題：對於某些字彙用法仍有疑慮，請多注意容易混淆的單字。

12 題以下：建議重新將本書單字及例句確實熟讀後，再做一次測驗。

認識
多益考試

　　TOEIC 多益測驗的全名為 Test of English for International Communication，也就是「國際溝通英語測驗」的簡稱，是專供母語非英語人士使用的英語能力測驗，測驗分數反映受測者在國際生活及職場環境中的英語溝通能力。TOEIC 測驗本身並沒有所謂的「通過」或「不通過」，而是客觀地將受測者的能力，以聽力 5～495 分、閱讀 5～495 分、總分 10～990 分的指標呈現，提供各個企業或學校做為評估依據，受測者也可依此設定學習的目標。

測驗內容

一般商務	契約、談判、行銷、銷售、商業企劃、會議
製造業	工廠管理、生產線、品管
金融／預算	銀行業務、投資、稅務、會計、帳單
企業發展	研究、產品研發
辦公室	董事會、委員會、信件、備忘錄、電話、傳真、電子郵件、辦公室器材、辦公室流程
人事	招考、雇用、退休、薪資、升遷、應徵與廣告
採購	比價、訂貨、送貨、發票
技術層面	電子、科技、電腦、實驗室與相關器材、技術規格
房屋／地產	建築、規格、購買、租賃、電力瓦斯服務
旅遊	火車、飛機、計程車、巴士、船隻、票務、時刻表、車站、機場廣播、租車、飯店、預訂、延遲與取消
聚會	商務／非正式午餐、宴會、招待、餐廳訂位
娛樂	電影、劇場、音樂、藝術、媒體
保健	醫藥保險、看醫生、牙醫、診所、醫院

測驗方式

　　多益測驗為紙筆測驗，考生用鉛筆在電腦答案卷上作答。考生閱讀題本，接著在答案卡上劃記回答。答題時間約為兩小時，但考試時考生尚須先填寫個人資料，並簡短的回答關於教育與工作經歷的問卷，因此真正待在考場內時間會較長，約 2 小時 30 分鐘。測驗題數共 200 題，皆為單選題，分為兩大部分：聽力與閱讀。

〈聽力部分〉

◆ 測驗英語聽力理解的程度。

◆ 包含 4 大題，共 100 個單選題，以 CD 播放考題，考生會聽到各種模擬實境不同狀況的問題，以及相關主題的直述句、問句、對話以及獨白，然後根據所聽到的內容回答問題，測驗時間約為 45 分鐘。

題　型	題　數
照片描述	10 題
應答問題	30 題
簡短對話	30 題（10 段對話，每段對話包含 3 個問題）
簡短獨白	30 題（10 段獨白，每段獨白包含 3 個問題）

〈閱讀部分〉

◆ 測驗英文閱讀理解的程度。

◆ 分為 4 大題，共 100 個單選題，考生須閱讀多種題材的文章，並回答相關問題，考生可依個人能力調配閱讀及答題速度，測驗時間為 75 分鐘。

題　型	題　數
單句填空	40 題
段落填空	12 題
單篇文章理解	28 題（7~10 篇短文，每篇 2~5 題）
雙篇文章理解	20 題（4 組短文，每組 5 題）

　　近年來，多益新增口說及寫作測驗，由於此兩項測驗並非必考，考生可視自己的需求決定是否選考。

英語能力指標

TOEIC 成績	英語溝通能力
905~990	英文能力十分近似於英語母語人士，能夠流暢有條理的表達意見、參與談話，主持英文會議，調和衝突並做出結論，語言使用上即使有瑕疵，亦不會造成理解上的困擾。
785~900	可有效地運用英文滿足社交及工作上所需，措辭恰當、表達流暢；但在某些特定情形下，如：面臨緊張壓力、討論話題過於冷僻艱澀時，仍會顯現出語言能力不足的情況。
605~780	可以英語進行一般社交場合的談話，能夠應付例行性的業務需求，參加英文會議，聽取大部分要點；但無法流利的以英語發表意見、作辯論，使用的字彙、句型也以一般常見為主。
405~600	英文文字溝通能力尚可，會話方面稍嫌辭彙不足、語句簡單，但已能掌握少量工作相關語言，可以從事英語相關程度較低的工作。
255~400	語言能力僅僅侷限於簡單的一般日常生活對話，無法做連續性交談，也無法用英文進行工作。
10~250	只能以背誦的句子進行問答而不能自行造句，尚無法將英文當作溝通工具來使用。

社交會面
Face to Face

How many words do you know?
你知道這些字的意思和用法嗎？

- [ ] acquaintance
- [ ] conducive
- [ ] hospitality
- [ ] impartial
- [ ] proximity
- [ ] salutation

● **accompany**

[ə`kʌmpənɪ]

(v.) 陪同，伴隨

Would you like us to **accompany** you on your way back home?

你是否希望我們陪你一起回家？

延伸字 escort, go out with, follow

— ● **accountability**

[ə͵kaʊntə`bɪlətɪ]

(n.) 負責任，
有義務

accountable. (a).

Since we're discussing the **accountability** here, I think you are also accountable.

既然我們正在討論責任歸屬，我認為你也需要負責任。

延伸字 responsibility, liability

---

acknowledge (v) 接受, 承認.

— ● **acknowledgment**

[ək`nɑlɪdʒ͵mənt]

(n.) 確認，認可，
收到通知

I am still waiting for the **acknowledgment** from the top.

我仍然在等待高層的確認。

延伸字 recognition, appreciation, confirmation

escort (v) 護送, 陪伴.
'ɛskɔrt

lɑːə'bɪlətɪ
[liability. (n) 責任
[liable + (aj) 有義務的.
[liable to 易於 ...... 的, 有 ...... 化傾向.

acquaintance

[əˋkwentəns]

(n.) 熟識，知識，理解

He is an **acquaintance** of mine. We've met a few years back.

他是我熟識的人。我們是在幾年前認識的。

延伸字 familiarity, awareness, understanding

acquaint (v) 使....了解

---

affiliate

[əˋfɪlɪˏet]

(v.) 接納，附屬，與…有關

Affiliate marketing is the process of using third parties to sell your products.

聯盟行銷是一種利用第三方來銷售產品的流程。

延伸字 associate, connect, incorporate

---

anniversary

[ˏænəˋvɝˊsərɪ]

(adj.) 週年的

(n.) 紀念日

The company is celebrating its 5 year **anniversary**.

這間公司正在慶祝成立滿五週年。

延伸字 ceremony, festival

---

appealing

[əˋpilɪŋ]

(adj.) 有魅力的，動人的

Your proposal is **appealing** for sure, but I am still not convinced.

你的提案確實非常具有吸引力，但是我仍然有疑慮。

延伸字 moving, charming

apply

一 ▶ **applicable**

[`æplɪkəbl]

(adj.) 適當的，
可實施的

We are still not sure if these results are **applicable** to the real world.
我們還不確定這些結果是否適用於實際環境。

延伸字 appropriate, suitable, relative

▶ **appreciation**

[ə͵priʃɪˋeʃən]

(n.) 欣賞，鑑賞，
賞識

He shows his **appreciation** of the show by clapping.
他用鼓掌來展現出自己對這場表演的讚賞。

(v) 評價
ə`prezl (v) appraise
延伸字 appraisal, gratitude (v) 感激

ə`prezl
(v)評價
(v) appraise

▶ **apprehensive**

[͵æprɪˋhɛnsɪv]

(adj.) 掛念的，
憂慮的

I am **apprehensive** about my future after I made a big mistake.
在我犯下大錯之後，我對我的未來感到憂慮。

延伸字 afraid, fearful, worried

(v) apprehend 理解 領會
(adj) apprehensible 句理解的

▶ **approach**

[əˋprotʃ]

(v.) 接近，靠近

Do you know what our competitor **approached** Kevin for?
你知道我們的競爭對手聯繫 Kevin 的原因嗎？

延伸字 advance, come near

7/19

▶ **attend**

[ə`tɛnd]

(v.) 參加，出席，前往，處理

Don't worry about it. I'll **attend** to the matter.

別擔心那件事，我會處理。

延伸字 be present, go to

attendence (n)

▶ **attire**

[ə`taɪr]

(n.) 穿著，服裝

Just wear your regular **attire** to this party, no worries.

你只要穿一般的服裝來參加派對就好，別擔心。

延伸字 dress, array *(v) 佈陣，扒伴，部署，妥功*

▶ **aware**

[ə`wɛr]

(adj.) 知道的，察覺的

We are **aware** of the current situation, and are resolving it right now.

我們明白目前的狀況，而且正在試著解決。

延伸字 knowing, conscious, realizing

▶ **beverage**

[`bɛvərɪdʒ]

(n.) 飲料

I need to go and buy some **beverages** for the party.

我需要去買點派對要喝的飲料。

延伸字 drink, liquor, *(n) 酒* *(v) 潛酌*

borrow

[`baro]

(v.) 借，借用

借入

Can I **borrow** your car? I need to practice first before getting a driver's license.

我能借你的車嗎？我在考駕照之前需要先練習一下。

延伸字 take, lend 借出

Can You lend me your car

---

carnival

[`karnəvl]

(n.) 嘉年華會

The **carnival** is in town. Let's go check it out.

嘉年華會在城裡開始舉辦了。我們去看看吧。

延伸字 fair, festival

---

cautious

[`kɔʃəs]

(adj.) 小心的，謹慎的

He is a very **cautious** man, so good luck persuading him.

他是一個很謹慎的人，想說服他應該有點困難。

延伸字 protective

coincide + with.
[koɪnˋsaɪd]
(v.) 符合，巧合

coincident (a)
coincidentally (av)

Our opinions did not **coincide** on this case.

我們針對這個案件所提出的意見並不相符。

延伸字 correspond, synchronize

sɪnˋkrənɪk
(a) 同步的，同時的

---

compose
[kəmˋpoz]
(v.) 組成，寫作，
　　編寫

I've been up all night trying to **compose** the perfect love song.

我整晚沒睡，試著寫出最完美的情歌。

延伸字 formulate, write, compile

(v.) 匯編

---

conducive
[kənˋdjusɪv]
(adj.) 有助的，
　　　有益的

This quiet office is really **conducive** for working.

這間安靜的辦公室對於工作上非常有幫助。

延伸字 profitable, favorable

ˋprafətəbl.
(a) 有益

---

congratulate
[kənˋgrætʃəˌlet]
(v.) 祝賀，賀喜

Let me **congratulate** you on buying your first house.

恭喜你買了你的第一間房子。

延伸字 applaud, praise, compliment

11/20

conservative
[kən`sɝvətɪv]
(adj.) 保守的，
謹慎的

Our new CEO's view of the market is a bit too **conservative**.

我們新任執行長對於市場的看法有點太過保守了。

延伸字 cautious, protective

---

contribution
[ˌkɑntrə`bjuʃən]
(n.) 貢獻

We thank you for all your **contribution** to our foundation.

我們感謝你對我們基金會所做出的一切貢獻。

延伸字 tribute, present, donation

---

convenience
[kən`vinjəns]
(n.) 方便，合宜

We choose a school near where we live for our son out of **convenience**.

我們為求方便而為兒子選擇了住家附近的學校。

延伸字 expedience, handiness

Ik`spidɪəns

(n) 權宜之我

---

coordinate
[ko`ɔrdnet]
(v.) 協調

We should **coordinate** our efforts and achieve our goal.

我們應該同心協力達成目標。

`sɪŋkrənaɪz

延伸字 synchronize, correlate, accommodate

(v) 使...協調，合齩

counterfeit

[ˈkaʊntɚˌfɪt]

(adj.) 假冒的，虛偽的

The bank clerk told me I had a counterfeit note.

銀行的行員告訴我，我有一張假鈔。

延伸字 copied, imitative, fake

imɪtetɪv (a) imitate

---

credit

[ˈkrɛdɪt]

(n.) 信用，信賴，榮譽

Our company has a great international credit.

本公司擁有良好的國際商譽。

延伸字 belief, trust, faith

---

culinary

[ˈkjulɪˌnɛrɪ]

(adj.) 烹飪的，廚房的

The culinary secret of this dish is miso.

這道餐點烹煮的秘訣就是味噌。

延伸字 dietary (n) *daɪəˈtɛrɪ. (a) 食譜、飲食的*

---

daringly *dare (v)*

[ˈdɛrɪŋlɪ]

(adj.) 大膽地，*膽敢* 毅然地

The girl jumped out of the plane daringly.

女孩勇敢地跳下了飛機。

延伸字 boldly, fearlessly

bold lɪ. (av) 大膽地

delighted
[dɪˈlaɪtɪd]
(adj.) 高興的，
　　　快樂的

Grandma was **delighted** to see all her grandchildren.
祖母非常高興能見到她所有的孫子。
延伸字 overjoyed, cheerful

---

deputy
[ˈdɛpjətɪ]
(n.) 副手，代理人

Mr. Smith is away, so our <u>deputy chairman</u> will be the person in charge.
史密斯先生不在，因此我們副董事長是負責人。
延伸字 representative, delegate, agent

*delegate (v) 委派
(n) 代表*

---

desire
[dɪˈzaɪr]
(v.) 要求，渴望

After several days of overtime, a little break is much **desired**.
連續加班許多天之後，最渴望的是能夠休息一下。
延伸字 wish, want, fancy, lust

---

dignity
[ˈdɪgnətɪ]
(n.) 威嚴，尊貴

He refused my help to retain his **dignity**.
他為了維持自己的尊嚴而拒絕接受我的幫助。
stateliness
延伸字 stateliness, noble bearing

(n) 尊嚴

7/21

discretionary

[dɪˋskrɛʃənˌɛrɪ]

(adj.) 任意的

discrete (a)
[dɪˋskrit] 分離

When the people have less **discretionary** funds, they tend to spend less money.

當人們手上可以任意花用的閒錢變少時，他們會傾向於減少消費。

延伸字 open

arbitrary árbəˌtrɛrɪ
(a) 隨意, 任意

---

discussion

[dɪˋskʌʃən]

(n.) 爭論，討論

We are not arguing. We're <u>merely</u> having a **discussion**.

我們並沒有吵架，只是在稍作討論而已。

延伸字 debate, dispute, disagreement

---

elegance

[ˋɛləgəns]

(n.) 優雅，雅緻，典雅

The curtain in the office is the CEO's idea. It's full of **elegance**.

辦公室內的窗簾是出自執行長的想法，窗簾上充滿了典雅的氣息。。

延伸字 style, beauty, luxury

---

empirical

[ɛmˋpɪrɪkl̩]

(adj.) 根據經驗的

empiric
經驗主義

Talking to actual people is much more **empirical** than reading a textbook.

比起閱讀課本，實際與人交談更能夠獲得實質的經驗。

延伸字 pragmatic, practical, provisional

(a) prəˋvɪʒən!
臨時性的

energize

[ˈɛnɚˌdʒaɪz]

(v.) 供給⋯能量，
激勵

The compliments from the president **energized** our whole team.

總理的稱讚激勵了我們全體團隊。

延伸字 strengthen, stimulate

---

entertainment

[ˌɛntɚˈtenmənt]

(n.) 娛樂，消遣

We need some form of **entertainment** after all the hard work.

努力做了這麼多工作後，我們需要來點娛樂。

延伸字 amusement, fun, recreation

---

episode

[ˈɛpəˌsod]

(n.) 一段節目，
情節

We all sat down and watched an **episode** of our favorite TV show.

我們全都坐下來，看了一集我們最愛的電視節目。

延伸字 occurrence, happening, experience

---

ethic

[ˈɛθɪk]

(n.) 倫理，道德
規範

Her actions in front of the press yesterday were far from **ethic**.

她昨天在媒體前的行為根本和倫理道德沾不上邊。

延伸字 virtue, integrity, fairness, morality

fair ca)

vɜtʃu integrətɪ

cn)美德 cn)試操

正直

express

[ɪk`sprɛs]

(v.) 表達，表示，
陳述

I bought him a bottle of wine to **express** my gratitude.

我買了一瓶葡萄酒給他，來表達我的感激。

延伸字 say, voice, describe

---

extraordinary

[ɪk`strɔrdn͵ɛrɪ]

(adj.) 特別的，
卓越的

Even an ordinary person can do **extraordinary** things.

就算是一個平凡人，也能有卓越的成就。

延伸字 special, unusual

---

familiar

[fə`mɪljɚ]

(adj.) 親近的，
親密的

This place looks **familiar**, but I don't think I've been here before.

這個地方看起來很眼熟，但是我不認為我來過這裡。

延伸字 friendly, close, personal, intimate

ɪn'tɚmet

(v.) 暗示
(a) 親密

---

fascinating

[`fæsn͵etɪŋ]

(adj.) 迷人的，
極美的

I find your trip to Thailand sounded very **fascinating**.

我認為你的泰國之旅聽起來非常迷人。

延伸字 adorable, charming

17/28

freelancer

[ˈfriˌlænsɚ]

(n.) 自由作家

His dream is to become a **freelancer**.

他的夢想是成為一位自由作家。

延伸字 specialist, expert

---

garment

[ˈgɑrmənt]

(n.) 衣服，服飾

There's a child alone in the **garment** store. She seems to be lost.

有一個小孩獨自一人在服飾店裡。她似乎迷路了。

延伸字 attire, apparel, clothes

---

glamorous

[ˈglæmərəs]

(adj.) 迷人的，
　　　富有魅力的

That dress is beautiful, and you look so **glamorous.**

那套洋裝真美麗，你看起來真迷人。

延伸字 attractive, charismatic, fascinating

---

glimpse

[glɪmps]

(n.) 一瞥

(v.) 看見，瞥見

I've caught a **glimpse** of the starlet during the parade.

我在遊行時瞥見了該名女星一眼。

延伸字 glance

hesitant

[ˈhɛzətənt]

(adj.) 遲疑的

He is a very **hesitant** person. It takes him ages to make up a decision.

他是一位非常不果決的人。他需要花很長的時間才能做出決定。

延伸字 diffident, backward

---

hospitality

[ˌhɑspɪˈtælətɪ]

(n.) 殷勤招待，好客

The farmer and his wife's **hospitality** made an impression on us.

農夫和他太太的好客，讓我們留下了深刻的印象。

延伸字 kindness, warmth

---

image

[ˈɪmɪdʒ]

(n.) 形象

Maintaining his or her **image** is often very important for a public figure.

對於公眾人物來說，保持形象通常是非常重要的。

延伸字 conception, impression, perception

---

impartial

[ɪmˈpɑrʃəl]

(adj.) 客觀的

Try and maintain an **impartial** view on the situation.

試著對於這種狀況保持客觀的立場。

延伸字 just, unbiased, fair

● imply

[ɪmˋplaɪ]

(v.) 暗示，啟發

I don't wish to **imply** that you are wrong.

我並沒有想要暗示你是錯的。

延伸字 suggest, hint, intimate

● impress

[ɪmˋprɛs]

(v.) 給…印象，
影響

His good performance **impressed** his boss a lot.

他良好的表現給了老闆非常深刻的印象。

延伸字 affect, strike

● individual

[ˌɪndəˋvɪdʒʊəl]

(adj.) 個人的，
個別的

We design our products according to **individual** needs.

我們依照客戶個別的需求來設計產品。

延伸字 single, separate, personal

● intention

[ɪnˋtɛnʃən]

(n.) 目的，目標，
意圖

To be honest, I doubt his **intention** is good.

老實說，我懷疑他的目的並不良善。

延伸字 purpose, goal, aim, intent

interact

[ˌɪntɚˋækt]

(v.) 互動

Nowadays young people like to use Facebook to **interact** with friends.

現在年輕人喜歡用「臉書」跟朋友互動。

延伸字 cooperate, network, connect

---

interactive

[ˌɪntɚˋæktɪv]

(adj.) 交互的，
　　　互相影響的

The kids all enjoyed the **interactive** math session.

孩子們非常喜歡互動式的數學課程。

延伸字 interactional

---

introduction

[ˌɪntrəˋdʌkʃən]

(n.) 介紹，引言，
　　 引進，傳入

On my first day, my manager asked me to do an **introduction** of myself to the team.

在我上班的第一天，主管要我向工作團隊做個自我介紹。

延伸字 commencement, foreword, preface

---

liberty

[ˋlɪbɚtɪ]

(n.) 自由，自由權

Every citizen has the **liberty** to speak their mind.

所有公民都有發表言論的自由。

延伸字 freedom, independence

luncheon
[ˈlʌntʃən]
(n.) 正式午餐會，
午宴

Our business associate invited us to a **luncheon** tomorrow.
我們生意上的夥伴邀請我們參加一場明天舉辦的午宴。

延伸字 lunch

---

marvelous
[ˈmɑrvələs]
(adj.) 了不起的，
令人驚異的

The performance at the circus is **marvelous**.
馬戲團的表演真是令人驚嘆。

延伸字 extraordinary, unbelievable, unimaginable

---

match
[mætʃ]
(n.) 比賽，競爭

The **match** score was tied, so the game went to overtime.
比賽分數拉平了，所以便進入延長賽。

延伸字 contest, battle, game

---

memorize
[ˈmɛməˌraɪz]
(v.) 背誦，記憶

He **memorized** all schedules of the week.
他將當週所有的行程都記下來了。

延伸字 remember

mindset

[ˋmaɪndˏsɛt]

(n.) 心態，傾向

Remember to always maintain a positive **mindset**.

記得隨時保持正面的心態。

延伸字 attitude, mentality

---

occur

[əˋkɝ]

(v.) 發生

Something unexpected **occurred**. Our partner is bankrupt.

意料之外的事發生了。我們的合作夥伴破產了。

延伸字 happen, transpire, take place

---

optimistic

[ˏɑptəˋmɪstɪk]

(adj.) 樂觀的，樂天的

You are always too **optimistic** when making business deals.

你談生意時總是過於樂觀。

延伸字 promising, encouraged, positive

---

originality

[əˏrɪdʒəˋnælətɪ]

(n.) 創造力，獨創性

Other than hard work, it's always good to have some **originality**.

除了工作認真之外，擁有獨創性也是非常好的。

延伸字 ingenuity, creativity

party

[ˋpɑrtɪ]

(n.) 聚會，黨派，
　　一夥人

I think it might be time to consider getting a third **party** involved in this.

我想應該是時候考慮找第三方來協助處理這件事了。

延伸字 group, company, gang

---

permission

[pəˋmɪʃən]

(n.) 允許，同意，
　　許可

I need the **permission** of the general manager first.

我需要先取得總經理的許可才行。

延伸字 permit, approval, license

---

persuasive

[pəˋswesɪv]

(adj.) 善說服的，
　　　口才好的

I can never refuse him; he is always so **persuasive**.

我從來沒辦法拒絕他，他的口才總是這麼的好。

延伸字 compelling, convincing, effectual

---

philosophy

[fəˋlɑsəfɪ]

(n.) 哲學，原理，
　　哲理

Her **philosophy** of life is very fascinating.

她的生活哲學非常令人著迷。

延伸字 conception, viewpoint, ideology

physical

[ˈfɪzɪkl̩]

(adj.) 身體的，
物質的

His **physical** health is great, but mentally he's really sick.

他的身體非常健康，但是精神上卻病得不輕。

延伸字 bodily, corporeal, fleshly, material

---

politician

[ˌpɑləˈtɪʃən]

(n.) 政治家，政客

The **politician** avoided all the questions and continued with his tour.

那位政客避答所有問題，並繼續他的參訪行程。

延伸字 diplomat

---

present

[ˈprɛznt]

(adj.) 在場的，
目前的

I can see that all the members of our team are **present**.

我看見我們團隊的所有成員都在場。

延伸字 now

---

profile

[ˈprofaɪl]

(n.) 輪廓，外型，
形象

I've heard Mary just won the lottery, but she's maintaining a low **profile** about it.

聽說 Mary 中了樂透，但她對這件事一直保持低調。

延伸字 outline, contour, shape

proximity

[prɑk`sɪmətɪ]

(n.) 接近，鄰近，親近

The new department store was opened in the **proximity** of our office.

新的百貨公司在我們辦公室附近開幕了。

延伸字 vicinity

---

recognition

[ˌrɛkəg`nɪʃən]

(n.) 認出，記起

After the earthquake, my school is almost out of **recognition**.

在地震之後，我幾乎認不出我的學校了。

延伸字 identification, recollection, recall

---

reject

[rɪ`dʒɛkt]

(v.) 拒絕，排除

My manager **rejected** the latest interviewee.

我的主管拒絕了最近的這位面試者。

延伸字 exclude, eliminate, expel

---

rely

[rɪ`laɪ]

(v.) 依賴，倚靠

I have to **rely** on others to achieve my goal.

我必須依賴別人才能達成我的目標。

延伸字 trust, confide, depend on

renowned

[rɪˋnaʊnd]

(adj.) 出名的，
有聲譽的

He is **renowned** for his talent in computer science.

他在資訊工程學上的天分使他變得赫赫有名。

延伸字 famous, popular, notable

---

resolution

[ˏrɛzəˋluʃən]

(n.) 決定，決心，
期望

Their new **resolution** is to sign a new agreement with their customer.

他們新的期望便是與客戶簽下新的合同。

延伸字 determination, resolve, decision

---

resonance

[ˋrɛzənəns]

(n.) 共鳴，迴響

The structure of this cave caused a lot of **resonance**.

這個洞穴的構造產生出許多共鳴。

延伸字 rapport

---

salutation

[ˏsæljəˋteʃən]

(n.) 招呼，寒暄，
問候

While writing a business email, it's best to learn the proper **salutations** first.

撰寫商務電子郵件時，最好先學習使用合乎禮儀的問候語。

延伸字 address, hello, bow

slant

[slænt]

(v.) 歪曲，傾斜

(n.) 偏見

Enough with your **slants**. Please focus on the important things.

不要再有偏見了。請專注在重要的事情上。

延伸字 tilt, lean

---

spouse

[spaʊz]

(n.) 配偶，同伴

Please put the name of your **spouse** on this form.

請在這張表格上填入你的配偶的姓名。

延伸字 mate, partner

---

status

[ˋstetəs]

(n.) 地位

Women's social **status** hasn't changed much over the years.

經過了這麼多年，女性的社會地位仍然沒有多大的改變。

延伸字 rank

---

strict

[strɪkt]

(adj.) 嚴格的，
刻板的

My father is very **strict** with our school performances.

我父親對於我們在學校的表現，要求非常嚴格。

延伸字 harsh, precise, stern

subjective

[səbˋdʒɛktɪv]

(adj.) 主觀的，
主觀上的

When an argument becomes too **subjective**, it's best to take a step back.

當爭論變得太過主觀時，最好先各退一步。

延伸字 nonobjective

---

tabloid

[ˋtæblɔɪd]

(n.) 小報，文摘

Don't believe everything the **tabloid** says.

別太相信那些小報報導的消息。

延伸字 sheet, condensation

---

tempt

[tɛmpt]

(v.) 吸引，引誘

Their high salary offer **tempted** Michael.

對方所提出的高薪條件非常吸引 Michael。

延伸字 attract, appeal, seduce

---

tremendous

[trɪˋmɛndəs]

(adj.) 巨大的，
極大的

With the rise in Internet social media, we should capture this **tremendous** force to create viral marketing.

隨著網路社群媒體熱潮興起，我們應該善用這波驚人的力量製造行銷話題。

延伸字 enormous, immense, vast

update
[ʌp`det]
(v.) 使…合乎時代
，更新

Our servers are currently **updating**, so please bear with us.

我們的伺服器目前正在更新，煩請見諒。

延伸字 replenish, renew

---

valuable
[`væljʊəbl̩]
(adj.) 值錢的，
有價值的

Stop with the chit chatting. We are wasting **valuable** time.

別再閒聊了，我們正在浪費寶貴的時間。

延伸字 expensive, priceless

---

vanity
[`vænətɪ]
(n.) 虛幻，自負，
虛榮心，

Don't let your **vanity** blind your judgment.

別讓你的虛榮心蒙蔽了判斷力。

延伸字 egotism, pride, self-worship

---

vital
[`vaɪtl̩]
(adj.) 重要的，
生命的

The person at the door claims to have **vital** information.

門口的那個人宣稱自己握有重要的資訊。

延伸字 necessary, significant, indispensable

volunteer

[ˌvɑlən`tɪr]

(n.) 自願參加者，義工

We are glad that so many **volunteers** showed up to help with the work.

我們很高興出現了許多自願協助完成工作的人。

延伸字 conscript

---

wrinkle

[`rɪŋkl]

(n.) 摺皺，皺紋

My boss' face was seamed with **wrinkles**. He is 75 years old now.

我老闆的臉上佈滿了皺紋。他已經 75 歲了。

延伸字 fold, ridge, crease

商業書信
Business Letters

2

How many words do you know?
你知道這些字的意思和用法嗎？

- ☐ authorize
- ☐ endorsement
- ☐ mandatory
- ☐ prioritize
- ☐ recipient
- ☐ template

abbreviation
[əˌbrivɪˋeʃən]
(n.) 縮短，省略，縮寫字

Young people nowadays love to use **abbreviations** to express feelings on the Internet.

現在的年輕人很喜歡在網路上用縮寫字來表達情緒。

延伸字 brief, abstract, synopsis

---

abstract
[ˋæbstrækt]
(n.) 摘要
(adj.) 抽象的

This painting is way too **abstract** for me to understand.

這幅畫對我而言太過抽象了，我看不懂。

延伸字 essence, compendium

---

accessible
[ækˋsɛsəbl̩]
(adj.) 可得到的，可使用的

Is your resort fully **accessible** to someone who uses a wheelchair?

請問飯店內有方便輪椅使用者的無障礙設施嗎？

延伸字 reachable, attainable, available

---

adequate
[ˋædəkwɪt]
(adj.) 足夠的

Your knowledge in accounting is **adequate** at least.

你對於會計的知識至少還算足夠。

延伸字 enough, sufficient

adhere

[əd`hɪr]

(v.) 堅持，附著

The poster has been **adhered** on that wall for a while.

那張海報已經黏在那面牆上一陣子了。

延伸字 cling, stuck

---

agreement

[ə`grimənt]

(n.) 同意，一致，協議

After some discussion, I think it's safe to say that we're all in **agreement**.

討論之後，我想我可以說我們已經一致同意了。

延伸字 bargain, contract, approval

---

anticipate

[æn`tɪsə͵pet]

(v.) 預期，預先

Our competitor has already **anticipated** our move.

我們的競爭對手早已預料到我們的策略。

延伸字 forecast, foresee, apprehend

---

appropriate

[ə`proprɪ͵et]

(adj.) 適當的，恰當的

When attending events, remember to wear the **appropriate** attire.

參與不同活動時，請記得穿著適當的服裝。

延伸字 suitable, fitting, proper

approve
[əˋpruv]
(v.) 贊成，准許，
認可

We are unable to **approve** your loan application this time.
此次我們無法核准您的貸款申請。

延伸字 accept, endorse, accredit

---

aspect
[ˋæspɛkt]
(n.) 方面，觀點

I was responsible for all **aspects** of store management, including sales, inventory, and overseeing the annual budget.
我負責店面管理的大小事，包括業務、庫存、監控年度預算。

延伸字 perspective, angle

---

assume
[əˋsjum]
(v.) 以為，假定，
認為

Judging by his accent, I **assume** he's from Germany.
根據他的口音來判斷，我認為他是從德國來的。

延伸字 suppose, presume, suspect

---

attachment
[əˋtætʃmənt]
(n.) 附著，附件，
附屬物

I have placed the file as an **attachment** on this email.
我將該檔案用附件的方式附在這封電子郵件內。

延伸字 connection, extension, supplement

authorize

[`ɔθəraɪz]

(v.) 授權，允許

I have been **authorized** to sign this agreement.

我被授權簽署這項協議。

延伸字 legalize, assign, give power to

---

autonomy

[ɔ`tɑnəmɪ]

(n.) 自治，自治權

People are protesting for more **autonomy**.

人們正在為爭取更多自治權而進行抗議。

延伸字 liberty, freedom

---

beforehand

[bɪ`for͵hænd]

(adv.) 事先，預先

I would really appreciate it if you could give me a heads up **beforehand**.

如果你能預先通知我一聲的話，我將會非常感激。

延伸字 ahead, earlier, in advance

---

cancel

[`kænsl̩]

(v.) 刪去，劃掉，取消

Since we are still stuck in traffic, we might have to **cancel** the reservation.

由於我們仍然被困在車陣之中，我們可能得取消預約了。

延伸字 erase, delete, obliterate

○ category
[`kætə͵gorɪ]

(n.) 種類，部屬，
　　類目

These two products are within different **categories**.

這兩項產品分別屬於不同的類別。

延伸字 class, type, variety

○ cautiously
[`kɔʃəslɪ]

(adv.) 小心地，
　　　謹慎地

Remember to make your financial decisions **cautiously**.

做財務決定時請記得謹慎為上。

延伸字 carefully

○ charge
[tʃɑrdʒ]

(v.) 將…記帳，
　　索價

Please **charge** this order to my Summit Bank Credit Card #123-456-789.

請將此款項記到我的 Summit 銀行信用卡帳上，卡號是 123-456-789。

延伸字 rate

○ clarify
[`klærə͵faɪ]

(v.) 澄清，闡明

We are happy to be able to **clarify** this matter for you.

我們很樂意向您澄清此事件的始末。

延伸字 explain, refine, make clear

classified ads

(n.) 分類廣告

I am checking through the **classified ads** to find a temporary job.

我正在從分類廣告裡尋找一份臨時的工作。

延伸字 classified advertising, classified advertisement

---

cognitive

[`kɑgnətɪv]

(adj.) 認知的，
感知的

This is a problem waiting to be solved by **cognitive** science.

這是一個必須由認知科學來解決的問題。

延伸字 comprehensible, intelligible

---

coherent

[ko`hɪrənt]

(adj.) 一致的，
協調的，
連貫的

We must come up with a **coherent** plan to improve our sales.

我們必須想出一個協調一致的計畫來提升銷售量。

延伸字 adherent, inseparable, fused

---

collateral

[kə`lætərəl]

(adj.) 並行的，
附帶的

Most of the time, **collateral** damage is caused by poor planning.

附帶損害大部分是因為計畫不良而造成的。

延伸字 corresponding, subordinate, concurrent

● **compelling**

[kəm`pɛlɪŋ]

(adj.) 強制的，
　　　引人注目的

That advertisement is very **compelling** indeed.

那個廣告確實非常引人注目。

延伸字 compulsory, imperative, fascinating

● **complementary**

[ˌkɑmplə`mɛntərɪ]

(adj.) 互補的，
　　　相配的

My sister and I have **complementary** personalities.

我妹妹和我個性互補。

延伸字 correlative, mutual, corresponding

● **complete**

[kəm`plit]

(v.) 完成，使齊全

Please let me know when you expect to **complete** the task.

請讓我知道你預計何時完成這項任務。

延伸字 finish, conclude, end

● **complexity**

[kəm`plɛksətɪ]

(n.) 複雜性

You cannot imagine the **complexity** of the situation.

你根本無法想像目前的狀況有多複雜。

延伸字 complication, intricacy

concentrate

[ˋkɑnsɛnˌtret]

(v.) 集中，全神
貫注

We **concentrated** all our efforts on this project.

我們投注了一切心血在這項企劃上。

延伸字 focus, think about

---

concise

[kənˋsaɪs]

(adj.) 摘要的，
簡潔的

He's very **concise** with his words.

他講話時非常簡潔扼要。

延伸字 brief, short

---

conclusion

[kənˋkluʒən]

(n.) 總結，結論

We have finally reached a **conclusion** of this agreement.

我們對這份協議總算有了結論。

延伸字 decision, ending, determination

---

confirm

[kənˋfɝm]

(v.) 確實，確定，
批准

Please kindly **confirm** your receipt and the mentioned deadline.

請您確認已接收到這項訊息，以及上述的截止時間。

延伸字 verify, prove, settle

○ **constantly**

[`kɑnstəntlɪ]

(adv.) 不斷地，
時常地

My neighbors are **constantly** fighting over little things.

我的鄰居不斷地為了一些小事在吵架。

延伸字 always, often, continually

○ **content**

[`kɑntɛnt]

(n.) 內容，要旨，
滿足

The **content** of this job requires me to be comfortable with crowds.

這份工作的內容要求我必須能夠自在面對人群。

延伸字 composition, constitution, satisfaction

○ **cornerstone**

[`kɔrnɚˌston]

(n.) 奠基石，基礎

I believe the success of this product will be the **cornerstone** of our future.

我相信這項產品的成功，將會成為我們未來發展的基礎。

延伸字 groundwork, keystone, foundation

- **correspondence**

  [ˌkɔrəˈspɑndəns]

  (n.) 相似，相近

  What you are telling me right now has little **correspondence** with what she told me.

  你現在告訴我的版本，跟她告訴我的非常不一樣。

  延伸字 similarity, analogy, likeness

- **credibility**

  [ˌkrɛdəˈbɪlətɪ]

  (n.) 可信度，
  確實性

  I'm afraid your words do not have **credibility** anymore.

  恐怕你所講的話再也沒有任何可信度了。

  延伸字 plausibility, probability

- **demonstrate**

  [ˈdɛmənˌstret]

  (v.) 證明，展示，
  示範

  May I make an appointment with you to **demonstrate** our latest line of products?

  我可以跟您約個時間，向您展示我們最新的產品嗎？

  延伸字 display, illustrate, show

- **diary**

  [ˈdaɪərɪ]

  (n.) 日記

  To help with his memory, the doctor suggests that he keep a **diary**.

  為了幫助他的記憶力，醫生建議他每天寫日記。

  延伸字 journal, log, record

● **discrepancy**

[dɪˋskrɛpənsɪ]

(n.) 差異，不同，
不一致

The accountant has found several **discrepancies** in the bills.

會計師在帳單上找到數個不一致的地方。

延伸字 inconsistency, variance, deviation

● **donation**

[doˋneʃən]

(n.) 捐款，捐贈

Thank you for your generous **donation** to the Help-Poor Foundation.

謝謝您對 Help-Poor 基金會的慷慨捐款。

延伸字 contribution, present, offering

● **elicit**

[ɪˋlɪsɪt]

(v.) 引出，誘出

She tried to **elicit** the truth of his whereabouts from me.

她試著引誘我說出他的下落。

延伸字 draw forth, get from

● **enclose**

[ɪnˋkloz]

(v.) 將（文件）封
入

Enclosed is a self-addressed stamped envelope for your reply.

內附回郵信封，方便您回覆。

延伸字 envelop, contain, include

endeavor

[ɪn`dɛvɚ]

(n.) 盡力，努力

This little **endeavor** of yours is pointless.

你的這點努力一點意義也沒有。

延伸字 effort, striving

---

endorsement

[ɪn`dɔrsmənt]

(n.) 簽名，贊同，背書

We've got the president's **endorsement** on this, so go ahead.

這件事情我們有總裁的認可，儘管進行吧。

延伸字 sign, approve, accredit

---

epicenter

[`ɛpɪˏsɛntɚ]

(n.) 震央，中心，集中點

Unfortunately, we are in the **epicenter** of this whole mess.

很不幸地，我們剛好位於這場災難的中心。

延伸字 center

---

fable

[`febḷ]

(n.) 寓言，虛構，傳說

Before mass printing technologies were invented, people relied on **fables** and stories to pass along histories.

在大規模列印技術發明前，人們依靠傳說和故事來傳述歷史。

延伸字 story, legend, fiction

formal

[`fɔrml̩]

(adj.) 正式的，
形式上的

Please remember to maintain your volume during a **formal** event.

在正式的場合中，請記得注意自己的音量。

延伸字 systematic, businesslike, arranged

---

format

[`fɔrmæt]

(n.) 版式，格式，
編排

After hours of discussion, we finally came up with a **format** that we all liked.

討論數小時之後，我們終於找到了一個大家都喜歡的版式。

延伸字 form, frame, structure

---

frequent

[`frikwənt]

(adj.) 慣例的，
頻繁的

I make **frequent** trips to Italy.

我經常前往義大利。

延伸字 common, prevalent, regular

---

guidance

[`gaɪdn̩s]

(n.) 指導，輔導

I'm wondering if you have the time to give us a little **guidance**.

我在想不知您是否有空可以給我們一些指教。

延伸字 instruction

handle

[`hændl]

(v.) 處理，指揮

I've taken on more projects than I can comfortably **handle**.

我負責的專案已經超出我的能力範圍。

延伸字 manage, direct, regulate

---

hesitate

[`hɛzəˌtet]

(v.) 猶豫，遲疑

If you require any further information, please do not **hesitate** to let me know.

若您還需要任何更進一步的資料，請隨時讓我知道。

延伸字 flounder, vacillate

---

highlight

[`haɪˌlaɪt]

(v.) 照亮，使顯著，使突出

Our party is **highlighted** by your presence.

妳的出席為我們的派對增添了更多光彩。

延伸字 focus, feature

---

identify

[aɪ`dɛntəˌfaɪ]

(v.) 確認，鑑別，鑑定

The experts are here to **identify** the source of the problem.

專家們是來這裡確認問題的根源。

延伸字 recognize, know, distinguish

inform
[ɪnˋfɔrm]
(v.) 通知，報告

I am writing to **inform** you that your order had been received on Monday.
我寫此信是要通知您，我們已於週一收到您的訂單。

延伸字 notify, acquaint, report

---

institute
[ˋɪnstətjut]
(v.) 建立，制定

The parliament just **instituted** a new law on drunk driving.
國會剛剛制定了一條新的酒駕法律。

延伸字 aggregate, incorporate

---

insurance
[ɪnˋʃurəns]
(n.) 保險，保險業，安全保障

It's wise to buy some car **insurance**, especially if it's a new one.
最好是幫車子買些保險，尤其是新車。

延伸字 surety, security, guaranty

---

integral
[ˋɪntəgrəl]
(adj.) 必須的，不可或缺的

That shipment is **integral** to the success of this deal.
那批貨物是這筆交易成功的必要條件。

延伸字 constituent, constitutional

jargon

['dʒɑrgən]

(n.) 行話，術語

When we write technical documents for the general public, we should avoid using computer **jargon**.

當我們在為一般大眾撰寫技術文件時，應避免使用電腦術語。

延伸字 tongue, vocabulary, terminology

---

journal

['dʒɜnl]

(n.) 日記，期刊，日誌

I always keep a **journal** during work to help arrange tasks into different priorities.

我工作時總是會在日誌上做記錄，協助我排定各項事務的優先順序。

延伸字 log, diary, magazine

---

letterhead

['lɛtə‚hɛd]

(n.) 信紙表頭

I am trying to find a graphic designer to design a new **letterhead** for our company.

我正在找一位平面設計師幫我們公司設計新的信紙表頭樣式。

延伸字 heading

---

logical

['lɑdʒɪkl]

(adj.) 合邏輯的，合理的

It's **logical** to think that they would accept this deal.

照理來說他們應該會接受這筆交易。

延伸字 reasonable, sensible, rational

商業書信

mandatory

[ˋmændəˌtorɪ]

(adj.) 命令的，強制的

During the start of the semester, we need to buy a lot of **mandatory** books.

學期開始，我們必須買很多指定用書。

延伸字 commanding, essential, compulsory

---

message

[ˋmɛsɪdʒ]

(n.) 信息，口信，音訊

The receptionist passed me several **message** slips when I walked into the office this morning.

我今天早上進辦公室時，總機小姐將許多電話留言的紙條交給了我。

延伸字 communication, note, word

---

miscellaneous

[ˌmɪsɪˋlenjəs]

(adj.) 各種的，雜項的

Our store offers a **miscellaneous** choice of goods.

我們的店面提供各式各樣的商品。

延伸字 varied, diversified, mixed

modify

[ˋmɑdəˌfaɪ]

(v.) 更改，改變

I've been trying to **modify** my lifestyle in order to be healthier.

為了讓自己更健康，我最近一直嘗試改變生活方式。

延伸字 change, alter

---

mutually

[ˋmjutʃʊəlɪ]

(adv.) 彼此，互相

I look forward to a **mutually** satisfying business relationship.

我期望能有雙方都滿意的業務合作關係。

延伸字 commonly

---

notice

[ˋnotɪs]

(n.) 公告，通知

(v.) 通知

My tenant has already missed his rent for 3 months. I am giving him the final **notice**.

我的房客已經三個月沒繳房租了。我準備要對他下最後通牒。

延伸字 note, regard, observe

---

occupy

[ˋɑkjəˌpaɪ]

(v.) 佔領，佔據，佔用

After the breakup, he **occupied** himself by playing video games all day long.

分手之後，他把整天的時間都拿來玩電玩遊戲。

延伸字 control, dominate, possess, take over

● **organize**

[ˋɔrgəˌnaɪz]

(v.) 組織，安排

We will **organize** a meeting to discuss details of this project.

我們會安排一個會議來討論此專案的細節。

延伸字 arrange, systematize, set up

● **outline**

[ˋautˌlaɪn]

(n.) 外形，輪廓，概要

The attached **outline** covers projected work through the end of the year.

附件內的大綱列出了整年度的預定工作。

延伸字 draft, profile, sketch

● **overdue**

[ˋovɚˋdju]

(adj.) 過期的，未兌的

I still have two **overdue** library books with me.

我還有兩本圖書館到期未還的書在手邊。

延伸字 outstanding, unsettled

● **overview**

[ˋovɚˌvju]

(n.) 概觀，概要，綜述

Mr. Chen gave us an **overview** of their latest project.

陳先生為我們提供了他們最新企劃案的概要。

延伸字 perspective

periodically

[pɪrɪˈɑdɪklɪ]

(adv.) 週期性地，
定期地

The security guards make their rounds **periodically**.

保全人員定時進行巡邏。

延伸字 regularly

---

prerequisite

[ˌpriˈrɛkwəzɪt]

(n.) 首要事物，
必要條件

You must fulfill the **prerequisite** first before taking the test.

你在接受測驗前必須先符合必要條件。

延伸字 requirement, necessity

---

prioritize

[praɪˈɔrəˌtaɪz]

(v.) 區分優先順序

We need to **prioritize** our goals in order to increase efficiency.

為了要提升效率，我們得先排定這些目標的優先程度。

延伸字 priority

---

progress

[prəˈgrɛs]

(v.) 進步，進行

Our plan has **progressed** to its last step.

我們的計劃已進展到最後一步。

延伸字 proceed, advance

prompt

[prɑmpt]

(adj.) 即時的，
迅速的

I am looking forward to your **prompt** reply.
我期待盡快收到您的回覆。

延伸字 quick, instant, immediate

---

proof

[pruf]

(n.) 證據，物證，
證明

The lack of reply is **proof** enough that he wasn't interested.
他一直沒有回應就是他沒興趣的證明。

延伸字 validation, evidence, confirmation

---

proofread

[`pruf͵rid]

(v.) 校對，校正

My manager always **proofreads** my business e-mails before I send them out.
我的業務電子郵件寄出去之前，我的主管都會先校對一遍。

延伸字 edit, correct, refine, revise

---

publish

[`pʌblɪʃ]

(v.) 出版，發行，
刊登

It's every writer's dream to get his / her book **published** one day.
每位作家的夢想，就是希望自己的書有朝一日能夠出版。

延伸字 reveal, circulate, broadcast

purchase
[`pɝtʃəs]
(n.) 購買，獲得

Thank you for your first **purchase** at IEG Hardware.
謝謝您首次光臨 IEG 五金店購物。

延伸字 buy, shop

---

receipt
[rɪ`sit]
(n.) 收到，收據

Please confirm **receipt** of this order by email, fax, or telephone.
請以電郵、傳真或電話方式確認您已收到此訂單。

延伸字 voucher, sales slip

---

recipient
[rɪ`sɪpɪənt]
(n.) 領受人，
接收者

When buying things online, remember to type in the correct **recipient** name to avoid delivery issues.
線上購物時，記得要輸入正確的收件者姓名，以避免寄送商品時發生問題。

延伸字 heir, beneficiary

---

recommendation
[ˌrɛkəmɛn`deʃən]
(n.) 推薦，建議

I am new to this town. Is there any **recommendation** for restaurants?
我才剛來到這個城鎮，有任何推薦的餐廳嗎？

延伸字 commendation, endorsement, suggestion

reflect
[rɪˋflɛkt]
(v.) 反射，照出，映出

The durability of our product **reflects** its fine craftsmanship.
我們產品的耐用性反映出它精良的製作工藝。
延伸字 mirror, send back

---

regardless
[rɪˋgɑrdlɪs]
(adv.) 不論如何

Regardless of the low pay, he still took the job.
儘管待遇相當低，他仍然接下了那份工作。
延伸字 notwithstanding, despite

---

regret
[rɪˋgrɛt]
(v.) 懊悔，遺憾

I **regret** to say that we are unable to assist you.
我很抱歉，我們無法協助您。
延伸字 bewail, be sorry for

---

regulatory
[ˋrɛgjələˌtorɪ]
(adj.) 管理的，控制的

You really should have a **regulatory** sleeping pattern.
你真的應該要控制好你的睡眠作息。
延伸字 administrative

remind
[rɪ`maɪnd]
(v.) 提醒，使想起

Just a note to **remind** you that we still haven't received the copy of the partnership contract.
此為提醒您，我們尚未收到合作結盟的合約書副本。
延伸字 prompt, reminisce

---

reminder
[rɪ`maɪndɚ]
(n.) 提示，催函，
提醒物

My colleague has put up a notice as a **reminder** for everyone to recycle.
我的同事貼了一張告示，提醒大家記得做回收。
延伸字 indication, suggestion, remembrance

---

reply
[rɪ`plaɪ]
(v.) 回答，回應

That customer hasn't yet **replied** to our new proposal.
那位客戶尚未對我們的新提案做出回應。
延伸字 answer, respond, acknowledge

---

representation
[ˌrɛprɪzɛn`teʃən]
(n.) 代表，代理

Our company has no **representation** in South America.
本公司在南美洲並沒有任何代理機構。
延伸字 portrait, trademark, expression

● **reserve**
[rɪˋzɝv]
(v.) 保存，保留，
　　預訂

I would like to **reserve** a non-smoking room in your hotel for three nights.
我想要訂一間非吸煙房，預計住三個晚上。
延伸字 keep, preserve, store

● **respective**
[rɪˋspɛktɪv]
(adj.) 各自的，
　　分別的

Please stay calm and return to your **respective** posts.
請保持鎮定並回到你們各自的崗位。
延伸字 particular, individual, separate

● **revise**
[rɪˋvaɪz]
(v.) 修訂，校訂，
　　修改

The assistant VP asked us to **revise** several terms on the contract.
協理要求我們修訂合約上的幾項條文。
延伸字 correct, change, improve

● **signature**
[ˋsɪgnətʃɚ]
(n.) 簽名，簽署，
　　特徵

I'm looking for Kyle. We need his **signature** in order to proceed.
我正在找 Kyle。我們需要他的簽名才能繼續進行。
延伸字 inscription, symbol, mark

spam

[spæm]

(n.) 垃圾郵件

Our server was hit with a **spam** attack; our engineer is trying to fix it.

我們的伺服器受到垃圾郵件攻擊，工程師正在試圖修復它。

延伸字 SPAM (Send Phenomenal Amounts of Mail), junk e-mail

---

stationery

[ˈsteʃənˌɛrɪ]

(n.) 信紙，文具

Our office is out of photocopy paper; it's time to hit the office **stationery** store.

辦公室的影印紙沒了，是時候去一趟辦公文具用品店了。

延伸字 writing paper

---

straightforward

[ˌstretˈfɔrwɚd]

(adj.) 簡單明瞭的

The product description should be **straightforward** and easy to read.

產品描述應該要簡單明瞭且容易閱讀。

延伸字 uncomplicated, unambiguous, forthright

---

strongly

[ˈstrɔŋlɪ]

(adv.) 強烈地

We **strongly** suggest Ms. Morgan review her insurance policy.

我們強烈建議 Morgan 小姐要檢視一下她的投保內容。

延伸字 completely, greatly, heavily

submit
[səb`mɪt]
(v.) 使服從，
使屈服，
提交

Mark **submitted** his proposal for media development to the board.
Mark 將他的媒體發展提案提交給董事會。

延伸字 yield, surrender, comply

---

summary
[`sʌmərɪ]
(n.) 總結，摘要

My boss asked me to give him a **summary** report of today's meeting.
我老闆要我交一份今天會議的摘要報告。

延伸字 abstract, abridgment, compendium

---

technically
[`tɛknɪklɪ]
(adv.) 技術上，
嚴格來說

The plan you proposed is **technically** feasible.
你所提議的計畫在技術上是可行的。

延伸字 strictly speaking

---

template
[`tɛmplɪt]
(n.) 樣板，模板，
型版

I am learning to build a bird cage by using a **template**.
我利用模板來學習如何搭建鳥籠。

延伸字 pattern

theory

[ˋθiərɪ]

(n.) 原理，推測

I have a **theory**, but I'll need further testing to prove it.

我目前有個推測，但是我還需要進一步實驗才能證明它。

延伸字 hypothesis, explanation

---

unacceptable

[ˌʌnəkˋsɛptəbl̩]

(adj.) 不可接受的

The language and tone of your last letter is **unacceptable** to us.

我們無法接受你上一封信裡的言詞和口吻。

延伸字 unsatisfactory, unpleasant

電話溝通
On the Phone

3

How many words do you know?
你知道這些字的意思和用法嗎？

☐ ambiguous
☐ decompression
☐ facilitate
☐ interruption
☐ verbally

absolute
[`æbsəˌlut]
(adj.) 完全的，
徹底的

There's no **absolute** standard for it.
它本身並沒有任何絕對的標準。

延伸字 complete, perfect

---

admission
[əd`mɪʃən]
(n.) 進入許可，
同意

The amount of **admission** fee they charged us for the show is way too ridiculous.
他們這場演出所收取的入場費用實在太誇張了。

延伸字 recognition, admittance

---

agenda
[ə`dʒɛndə]
(n.) 待辦事項，
議程

I've asked my secretary to type out today's **agenda**.
我要求秘書將今天的待辦事項打字出來。

延伸字 schedule, program, plan

---

ambiance
[`æmbɪəns]
(n.) 氣氛，情調

I really like the **ambiance** of your new restaurant.
我很喜歡你這間新餐廳的氣氛。

延伸字 atmosphere

ambiguous

[æm`bɪgjuəs]

(adj.) 含糊的，
不分明的

My manager's instructions have always been very **ambiguous**.

我主管的指示總是非常不清楚。

延伸字 unclear

---

articulate

[ɑr`tɪkjəlɪt]

(adj.) 口才好的，
發音清楚的

John is the most **articulate** person in the team.

John 是整個團隊中最會說話的。

延伸字 expressive, understandable, intelligible

---

assignment

[ə`saɪnmənt]

(n.) 任務，工作

Even though I'm off on vacation tomorrow, he still hands me an **assignment**.

雖然我明天就要去度假了，他仍然指派了一項工作給我。

延伸字 job, task, errand

---

attention

[ə`tɛnʃən]

(n.) 專心，注意，
注意力

After 8 hours of working, my **attention** is starting to fade.

工作了八個小時之後，我的注意力開始渙散了。

延伸字 consideration, concern

boardroom

[`bord͵rum]

(n.) 會議室

If you want to use the **boardroom**, please remember to sign up first.

如果你要使用會議室，請記得先登記。

延伸字 conference room

---

consensus

[kən`sɛnsəs]

(n.) 一致，共識

We have reached a general **consensus** towards your punishment.

針對你的懲處，我們已經達到基本的共識。

延伸字 agreement, unanimity

---

critical

[`krɪtɪkl]

(adj.) 關鍵性的，
　　　緊要的

That file is **critical** to our whole plan.

那份檔案對我們整項計劃非常重要。

延伸字 crucial, urgent, pressing

---

cyberspace

[`saɪbɚ͵spes]

(n.) 電子世界，
　　　虛擬世界

Nowadays, people are spending more and more time within **cyberspace**.

現今人們花在虛擬世界的時間越來越多。

延伸字 communications

decompression

[ˌdikəmˈprɛʃən]

(n.) 減壓

After entering the space station, the astronaut entered a **decompression** process.

在進入太空站之後，該名太空人開始進行減壓流程。

延伸字 looseness

---

distraction

[dɪˈstrækʃən]

(n.) 分心，娛樂，
　　分心的事物

I need some **distraction** to help me forget about work.

我需要其他能讓我分心的事物，才不會再想工作的事。

延伸字 interference, interruption, entertainment

---

disturb

[dɪsˈtɝb]

(v.) 妨礙，打擾

I am trying to enjoy some "me" time. Please don't **disturb** me.

我正在試著享受屬於自己的時間，請不要打擾我。

延伸字 annoy, bother, irritate

dull
[dʌl]
(adj.) 乏味的，
　　　無聊的

I think I need to be a bit more adventurous;
my life is too **dull**.

我覺得自己應該要再勇於冒險一點，我的
人生太乏味了。

延伸字 boring, uninteresting, dry

---

duplicate
[`djuplə͵kɪt]
(adj.) 複製的，
　　　一樣的
(n.) 複製品

The articles you submit should be original,
and there should be no **duplicate**
contents.

您提交的文章必須是原創的，不應該有內
容雷同的狀況。

延伸字 repeat, copy, reproduce

---

expire
[ɪk`spaɪr]
(v.) 到期，屆滿，
　　 終止

That jar of pickles has already **expired**.
Don't eat it.

那罐酸黃瓜已經過期了，不要吃。

延伸字 cease, vanish, end

extension

[ɪk`stɛnʃən]

(n.) 伸展，擴大，
延期，分機

Time is running out; we should ask for an **extension**.

時間快沒了，我們應該要求延長時間。

I can be reached at **extension** number 321.

你可以打分機 321 找到我。

延伸字 spread, sprawl, expansion

---

facilitate

[fə`sɪlə‚tet]

(v.) 促進，幫助，
使容易

He is the one who **facilitated** the cooperation between our two companies.

他就是那位促成我們兩家公司合作的人。

延伸字 ease, help, assist

---

gloom

[glum]

(n.) 憂鬱，幽暗

My friend is really down right now, and he thinks his future is filled with **gloom**.

我朋友現在很沮喪，他認為他的未來一片黑暗。

延伸字 unhappiness, somberness, oppression

harmony

[`harmənɪ]

(n.) 和諧，融洽，協調

Maintaining **harmony** within workplaces is important.

維持工作場所的融洽是很重要的。

延伸字 togetherness, consistency, cooperation

---

indicate

[`ɪndəˌket]

(v.) 顯示，象徵，指出

The forecast **indicates** there will be a storm coming.

天氣預報顯示即將會有暴風雨來襲。

延伸字 reveal, explain, disclose

---

interruption

[ˌɪntə`rʌpʃən]

(n.) 打岔，中斷

Is it too much to ask to let me finish without any **interruption**?

我只希望能在不被打岔的情況下講完話，這樣算要求很多嗎？

延伸字 dissolution, disturbance, disruption

---

objective

[əb`dʒɛktɪv]

(n.) 目的，目標

Don't let this problem hold you back; remember the **objective**.

別讓這項問題阻撓了你，記得你的目標。

延伸字 intention, goal, target

procedure

[prə`sidʒɚ]

(n.) 程序，步驟，手續

There is no need to rush. Please follow the **procedure**.

您不需要那麼急，請按照程序來進行。

延伸字 operation, strategy, practice

---

randomly

[`rændəmlɪ]

(adv.) 任意地，隨機地

The performers for our year-end party were chosen **randomly**.

我們年終晚會的表演者是隨機挑選出來的。

延伸字 arbitrarily, at random, indiscriminately

---

regarding

[rɪ`gardɪŋ]

(prep.) 就…而論，關於

Regarding this project, we might need a few more hours to complete.

關於這項企劃，我們可能還需要幾個小時才能完成。

延伸字 about

---

respond

[rɪ`spand]

(v.) 作答，回答

When asked about the recent scandal, the principle refused to **respond**.

當被問到近日的醜聞時，那位校長拒絕回答。

延伸字 answer, reply, retort

supply

[sə`plaɪ]

(v.) 供應，提供

Our vendor **supplied** us with various raw materials.

我們的供應商提供了我們各種原料。

延伸字 furnish, provide, store

---

switchboard

[`swɪtʃ͵bord]

(n.) 配電盤，
　　接線總機

The company decided to switch to an automated **switchboard** system to lower the cost.

公司決定改用自動化總機系統來降低開銷。

延伸字 operator

---

teleconference

[`tɛlə͵kɑnfərəns]

(n.) 電訊會議，
　　線上會議

Since most of our clients are based overseas, we have to regularly attend **teleconferences**.

由於我們大部分的客戶都在海外，因此我們必須經常開電訊會議。

延伸字 webinar

telemarketing

[ˌtɛləˈmɑrkɪtɪŋ]

(n.) 電話銷售

Telemarketing is a common way of discovering potential customers.

電話銷售是發掘潛在客戶的普遍方式。

延伸字 telesales, inside sales

---

thorough

[ˈθɝo]

(adj.) 徹底的，完全的

We are really happy with our cleaner. She is very **thorough**.

我們對於我們請的清潔工非常滿意。她打掃的非常徹底。

延伸字 complete, full

---

transfer

[trænsˈfɝ]

(v.) 轉接，轉換

Please hold on while I **transfer** your call to the accounting department.

請稍候，我為您轉接到會計部門。

延伸字 hand over, switch, pass

---

urge

[ɝdʒ]

(v.) 催促，力勸

She **urges** me to go take the certification exam.

她力勸我去參加認證考試。

延伸字 plead, advice, press

● urgent

[ˋɝdʒənt]

(adj.) 緊急的，
迫切的

Dave just passed me without saying hello.
I wonder what is so **urgent**?

Dave 剛剛經過我身邊，連聲招呼都沒有
打，不知道有什麼緊急的事情？

延伸字 compelling, immediate, pressing

● verbally

[ˋvɝblɪ]

(adv.) 言詞上，
口頭地

Since the Internet is down, I decide to brief
my team **verbally**.

由於網路斷線了，我決定口頭向我的團隊
做簡報。

延伸字 orally

4

出差商旅
Business Traveling

How many words do you know?
你知道這些字的意思和用法嗎？

- [ ] aviation
- [ ] circulation
- [ ] denomination
- [ ] excursion
- [ ] itinerary
- [ ] tenant

MP3
18

accreditation

[əˌkrɛdəˋteʃən]

(n.) 信賴，委派，
鑑定

Our new factory is currently under the government's **accreditation** process.

我們的新廠房目前正在接受政府的認證流程。

延伸字 commission, appointment, authorization

---

agent

[ˋedʒənt]

(n.) 代理人，
仲介人

Ticket bookings can be done through an **agent**, travel website or through an airline.

旅客可以透過旅行社、旅遊網站或航空公司訂票。

延伸字 operator, worker

---

amateur

[ˋæməˌtʃʊr]

(adj.) 業餘的，
外行的

All members of our photography club are enthusiastic **amateurs.**

我們攝影社的所有成員都是充滿熱忱的業餘愛好者。

延伸字 apprentice, learner, dilettante

annually
[ˋænjʊəlɪ]
(adv.) 每年一次

Your really should have your teeth checked **annually** at least.
你真的應該至少一年要檢查一次你的牙齒。

延伸字 yearly

---

appointment
[əˋpɔɪntmənt]
(n.) 任命，選派，約會

I am ready to accept the **appointment** as the next director.
我已經準備好接任下一任的總監職務了。

延伸字 designation, representative, invitation

---

assemble
[əˋsɛmbḷ]
(v.) 集合，聚集

I'm **assembling** everyone tomorrow morning for a quick meeting.
我明天早上要集合大家很快地開個會。

延伸字 meet, collect, congregate

---

attendance
[əˋtɛndəns]
(n.) 出席人數，出席

Could you help me count the **attendance** of this seminar?
你能幫我計算一下這場研討會的出席人數嗎？

延伸字 appearance, participation, presence

attraction
[ə`trækʃən]
(n.) 樂見之事物，吸引力

For overall information about New York, including accommodation and **attractions**, contact the NY Visitors Authority.

欲取得關於紐約的全部資訊，包括飯店和景點介紹，請洽紐約遊客中心。

延伸字 allurement, enchantment, interest

---

audience
[`ɔdɪəns]
(n.) 聽眾，觀眾

His speech had an electric effect on the **audience**.

他的演說使聽眾感到非常震撼。

延伸字 spectators, viewers

---

automatic
[͵ɔtə`mætɪk]
(adj.) 自動的

Our president bought an **automatic** coffee machine for us to use in the office.

我們董事長買了一台自動咖啡機，放在辦公室裡讓我們使用。

延伸字 spontaneous, self-acting, self-working

---

aviation
[͵evɪ`eʃən]
(n.) 航空，飛行

He has been into **aviation** since he was a kid.

他從小就對航空相關領域非常感興趣。

延伸字 aerodynamics, flight

baggage

[ˈbægɪdʒ]

(n.) 行李，包袱

I am at the **baggage** claim area waiting for my luggage.

我正在行李提領處等候我的行李。

延伸字 luggage, pack, backpack

---

beneficiary

[ˌbɛnəˈfɪʃərɪ]

(n.) 受益人，
受惠者

I have placed my daughter as my **beneficiary**.

我指定我的女兒做我的受益人。

延伸字 successor, receiver

---

booking

[ˈbʊkɪŋ]

(n.) 預約，登記

The hotel lost our **booking**, so they upgraded us to the deluxe suite.

由於飯店弄丟了我們的訂房記錄，因此將我們的房間升級為豪華套房。

延伸字 register

---

burnout

[ˈbɝnˌaʊt]

(n.) 精疲力盡，
燃油耗盡

After 8 years as a nurse, Hank started to feel like a **burnout**.

在擔任八年護理師的工作之後，Hank 開始感到精疲力盡。

延伸字 exhaustion

○ **bustling**

[`bʌslɪŋ]

(adj.) 繁忙的，
　　　熙來攘往的

The street is **bustling** with tourists.
街道上滿是觀光客。

延伸字 busy

○ **cancellation**

[ˌkænsḷ`eʃən]

(n.) 取消，作廢

If you somehow change your mind, you
will have to pay a **cancellation** fee.
如果您改變主意的話，就必須支付一筆取
消費用。

延伸字 dissolution, recall

○ **celebrate**

[`sɛləˌbret]

(v.) 慶祝，祝賀

Congratulations on your promotion! Let's
celebrate.
恭喜你升職，我們來慶祝一下吧。

延伸字 proclaim, praise

○ **ceremony**

[`sɛrəˌmonɪ]

(n.) 典禮，儀式，
　　禮儀

We will be holding a small wedding
ceremony at the church.
我們將在教堂舉辦一場小型的結婚典禮。

延伸字 conformity, function, rite

---

circulation

[ˌsɛkjəˈleʃən]

(n.) 流通，發行量

Our newsletter has a **circulation** of over a million.

我們的電子報有超過一百萬的發行量。

延伸字 dissemination

---

concierge

[ˌkɑnsɪˈɛrʒ]

(n.) 服務櫃台，
門房

If you want to rent a cell phone during your stay, have the hotel **concierge** obtain one for you.

如果你住宿期間需要租手機，可以向飯店櫃台人員申請。

延伸字 attendant, doorman, porter

---

continent

[ˈkɑntənənt]

(n.) 大陸，陸地，
大洲

After a few months on the sea, it's good to be back on the **continent**.

待在海上好幾個月之後，能回到陸地上真好。

延伸字 mainland

---

copyright

[ˈkɑpɪˌraɪt]

(n.) 版權，著作權

We own the **copyright** of that image.

我們擁有那個影像的版權。

延伸字 license, patent

currently

[`kɝəntlɪ]

(adv.) 現在，當前

She is **currently** unavailable. Can I take a message?

她目前無法接聽。我能幫您留個言嗎？

延伸字 now, presently

---

delegate

[`dɛlə‚get]

(n.) 代表，委員

(v.) 委派

Mr. Huang could not make it today, so he sent me as his **delegate**.

黃先生今天無法與會，所以他派我以代表的身分前來。

延伸字 representative, deputy, commission, authorize

---

deluxe

[dɪ`lʌks]

(adj.) 豪華的，高級的

The company reserves **deluxe** rooms for foreign sponsors.

公司將豪華的房間預留給國外的贊助廠商。

延伸字 superior, magnificent

---

denomination

[dɪ‚namə`neʃən]

(n.) 貨幣面額，單位

US bank notes come in **denominations** as low as $1 and as high as $100.

美國的紙鈔面額最小是一元，最大是一百元。

延伸字 value, measure

depart

[dɪ`part]

(v.) 啟程，出發，離去

When will the train **depart**? It's already 5 minutes past the departure time.

火車什麼時候才要出發？已經超過發車時間五分鐘了。

延伸字 leave, exit, withdraw

---

deplete

[dɪ`plit]

(v.) 用盡，使減少

The resources of Earth are **depleting** very fast.

地球的資源正在迅速地減少。

延伸字 deflate, lessen

---

destination

[ˌdɛstə`neʃən]

(n.) 目的地，終點

I am just passing through here. My **destination** is a town further north.

我只是路過這裡而已。我的目的地是更北方的一個城鎮。

延伸字 end, goal, objective

---

devastation

[ˌdɛvəs`teʃən]

(n.) 荒廢，摧殘

The **devastation** of the typhoon is very horrifying.

颱風的肆虐非常可怕。

延伸字 havoc, destruction

directory

[dəˋrɛktərɪ]

(n.) 指南，手冊，名錄

I am buying a car for the first time, so my friend suggests that I go get a car **directory** first.

我是第一次買車，所以朋友建議我先去索取一本汽車型錄。

延伸字 record, index, register

---

display

[dɪˋsple]

(v.) 陳列，展出，表現

We are still trying to figure out the best way to **display** our product.

我們還在試著想出陳列產品的最佳方式。

延伸字 demonstrate, exhibit, show

---

distribution

[ˌdɪstrəˋbjuʃən]

(n.) 分發，銷售，分佈

Can you give me the age **distribution** of our target audience?

你能給我我們目標族群的年齡分佈嗎？

延伸字 arrangement, dissemination, organization

domestic

[dəˋmɛstɪk]

(adj.) 家庭的，
國內的

International brands products are not always better than products from **domestic** brands.

國際品牌的產品並不一定比國內品牌的產品來的好。

延伸字 internal

---

downshift

[ˋdaʊnʃɪft]

(v.) (n.) 減速

I try to **downshift** to slow down, since it lowers my blood pressure.

我試著放慢步調，因為可以降低我的血壓。

延伸字 decelerate, retard

---

dramatic

[drəˋmætɪk]

(adj.) 戲劇性的，
引人注目的

As you enter the Copper Valley from Anchorage, the **dramatic** Wrangell Mountains are right in front of you.

當你從安克拉治進入庫柏谷地，引人注目的蘭格爾山脈就在你眼前。

延伸字 striking, exciting, vivid

---

duration

[djʊˋreʃən]

(n.) 期間

The **duration** of the meeting is two hours.

會議時間為兩小時。

延伸字 time, period, term

● earmark
[`ɪr͵mɑrk]
(v.) 標記
(n.) 特徵，記號

You should **earmark** the job you would like to get, before you start searching.
你在開始尋找工作前，應該將你想要的工作類型標記起來。

延伸字 distinction, attribute, trademark

● embarkation
[͵ɛmbɑr`keʃən]
(n.) 乘坐，從事

We shall be starting the **embarkation** tomorrow.
我們將在明天開始登船。

延伸字 departure

● emerge
[ɪ`mɝdʒ]
(v.) 出現，顯露

After the rain, the grasses **emerged** from the soil.
下雨之後，青草全都從泥土中長了出來。

延伸字 appear, rise

● emerging
[ɪ`mɝdʒɪŋ]
(adj.) 新興的

Cloud computing is an **emerging** technology which is likely to have a bright future.
雲端科技是一項很有可能在未來大放異彩的新興技術。

延伸字 rising, developing

entice

[ɪn`taɪs]

(v.) 誘使，慫恿

Many of the big hotels along Grand Avenue put on free shows to **entice** people in.

格蘭大道上的許多大飯店都提供免費表演，以吸引顧客上門。

延伸字 attract, lure, tempt

---

entitlement

[ɪn`taɪt!mənt]

(n.) 應得之權利

I really don't like his sense of **entitlement**.

我很不喜歡他一副「那都是我應得的」的態度。

延伸字 right

---

etiquette

[`ɛtɪkɛt]

(n.) 禮節，禮儀，成規

Please keep in mind that this is a formal event, and watch your **etiquette**.

請記得這是一個正式場合，請注意你的禮儀。

延伸字 courtesy, manner

---

excursion

[ɪk`skɝʒən]

(n.) 短程旅行，出遊

We are planning for our **excursion** next month. We are going to Hawaii!

我們正在計劃下個月的旅行。我們準備要去夏威夷！

延伸字 trip, journey, tour

exposition

[ˌɛkspəˋzɪʃən]

(n.) 展覽會，
博覽會

Our company will definitely be present at this year's **exposition**.

我們公司一定會參與今年的博覽會。

延伸字 presentation, expo, demonstration

---

external

[ɪkˋstɝnəl]

(adj.) 外部的，
表面的

For this problem, we might have to find someone **external** to resolve it.

針對這項問題，我們可能得找外部人員來解決它。

延伸字 outside, outer, surface

---

footprint

[ˋfʊtˌprɪnt]

(n.) 腳印，足跡

The burglar left a set of **footprints** at the doorway.

小偷在走廊留下了一雙腳印。

延伸字 imprint, track, impression

---

forecast

[ˋforˌkæst]

(v.) (n.) 預測，預報

The **forecast** for the next 24 hours is clear throughout the day.

接下來 24 小時的天氣預測為全天晴朗。

延伸字 predict, foretell, foresee

- **frontier**
  [frʌn`tɪr]
  (n.) 新領域，國境

  With this product, our company is venturing into a new **frontier**.
  藉由這項產品，本公司即將進入一個全新的領域。
  延伸字 border, outskirts

- **headquarters**
  [`hɛd`kwɔrtɚz]
  (n.) 總部，指揮部

  Ken has been called back to the **headquarters** to brief the board.
  Ken 被召回總部向董事會做簡報。
  延伸字 base, main office

- **hurricane**
  [`hɝɪˌken]
  (n.) 暴風，颶風

  Scientists track **hurricanes** as they approach land.
  科學家在暴風接近陸地時就開始追蹤。
  延伸字 storm, tornado, cyclone

- **hydrated**
  [`haɪdretɪd]
  (adj.) 含水的

  Staying **hydrated** is one of the most important things to do when you are camping and hiking.
  露營或登山時，補充水份是最重要的事項之一。
  延伸字 watered

● hypermarket
[ˌhaɪpɚˋmɑrkɪt]
(n.) 大超市

Local grocery stores are affected a lot by the new **hypermarket**.

新開的大超市對當地的雜貨店造成了很大的影響。

延伸字 supermarket

● industry
[ˋɪndəstrɪ]
(n.) 商業，企業

Our product is guaranteed the **industry's** best.

我們的產品保證是業界第一。

延伸字 trade, business

● ingredient
[ɪnˋgridɪənt]
(n.) 組成部分，
要素

There is a list of **ingredients** on the side of the package.

包裝的側邊有標示成分的清單。

延伸字 part, element

● innovative
[ˋɪnəˌvetɪv]
(adj.) 創新的

Our company's success is mainly due to our CEO's **innovative** ideas.

本公司的成功主要歸功於我們執行長的創新想法。

延伸字 state-of-the-art, inventive, new

intersection

[ˌɪntɚˈsɛkʃən]

(n.) 交叉路口

In the US, service stations are usually located at the **intersections** of major highways.

在美國，加油服務站通常位在主要公路的交叉口。

延伸字 junction, crossway

---

invitation

[ˌɪnvəˈteʃən]

(n.) 招待，邀請，請帖

Did you get an **invitation** to the party next week?

你收到下週那場派對的邀請函了嗎？

延伸字 attraction, temptation

---

itinerary

[aɪˈtɪnəˌrɛrɪ]

(n.) 旅程，路線，旅行計畫

Our travel agent mailed us the **itinerary** of our trip.

我們的旅行社把行程表寄給了我們。

延伸字 agenda, route

---

leisure

[ˈliʒɚ]

(n.) 空閒時間，閒暇

She used her **leisure** time to improve her English.

她利用閒暇時間來提升英語能力。

延伸字 free time, spare time

> **liberate**
> [ˈlɪbəˌret]
> (v.) 解放，使自由

The criminal was **liberated** after 10 years of imprisonment.

那位罪犯被監禁十年之後，終於獲得自由了。

延伸字 free, deliver, release

> **lobby**
> [ˈlɑbɪ]
> (n.) 大廳，門廊

I have asked the delivery man to wait for me in the **lobby**.

我要求送貨員在大廳等我。

延伸字 entrance, passageway, hall

> **medical**
> [ˈmɛdɪkl̩]
> (adj.) 醫療的，內科的

New Jersey has excellent **medical** services, but as in the rest of the US, they are very expensive.

紐澤西州有絕佳的醫療服務，但就像美國其他州一樣，費用是很昂貴的。

延伸字 healing, therapeutic

merchant

[ˋmɝtʃənt]

(n.) 商人，零售商

The **merchant** is unhappy with the situation of his business.

那位商人對於目前的生意狀況不是很滿意。

延伸字 trader, salesman, dealer

---

obtain

[əbˋten]

(v.) 獲得，得到

Weather information can be **obtained** from information stations, and through reports on radio.

我們可以透過資訊站，或聽廣播獲得氣象資訊。

延伸字 acquire, gain, receive

---

on display

陳列，展示

We have our latest model **on display** over there.

我們將最新型號的產品陳列在那裡。

延伸字 exhibit, showcase

---

outsource

[ˋautˏsɔrs]

(v.) 委外提供服務，外包

Our company decided to **outsource** some of the work to reduce our workload.

我們公司決定將一些工作外包，減輕我們的工作量。

延伸字 subcontract

● **overpopulated**

[͵ovɚˋpɑpjəˌletɪd]

(adj.) 人口過多的

An **overpopulated** city will have many problems.

一座人口過多的城市一定會有許多問題。

延伸字 occupied, swarming

● **overseas**

[ˋovɚˋsiz]

(adj.) 海外的，
國外的

I've been waiting for my **overseas** package for weeks now.

我已經等這個來自海外的包裹好幾個禮拜了。

延伸字 foreign

● **package**

[ˋpækɪdʒ]

(v.) 包裝，打包

(n.) 包裹

As the holiday season draws near, the workers are all busy **packaging** goods.

隨著假期的接近，員工們全都忙於包裝商品。

延伸字 container, bunch

● **participate**

[pɑrˋtɪsəˌpet]

(v.) 參加，參與

They decided to **participate** in the competition.

他們決定參加競賽。

延伸字 partake, take part in, join in

pastime

[ˋpæsˌtaɪm]

(n.) 消遣，娛樂

Bird watching is a popular **pastime** in Arizona, especially in spring, early summer, and fall.

賞鳥在亞利桑那州是很受歡迎的休閒活動，尤其是在春天、初夏和秋天。

延伸字 recreation, enjoyment, relaxation

---

personnel

[ˌpɝsṇˋɛl]

(n.) 人員，員工

If you need to send international telegrams, ask hotel **personnel** where to find the nearest Western Union Office.

若你需要傳送國際電報，可以向飯店人員詢問最近的西聯辦事處地點。

延伸字 staff, manpower, crew

---

precaution

[prɪˋkɔʃən]

(n.) 預防，警惕，謹慎

Taipei is a relatively safe place as long as some general **precautions** are observed.

只要事先做好安全防範，台北是一個相當安全的地方。

延伸字 safeguard

● **produce**

[prə`djus]

(v.) 生產，創造，製作

The new office setting **produced** better productivity.

辦公室新的空間配置，創造了更高的生產力。

延伸字 make, generate, create

● **quadruple**

[`kwɑdrʊpl]

(v.) 成為四倍

(adj.) 四倍的

Hotel room rates can more than **quadruple** when there is a major convention at the hotel.

當有大型研討會在該飯店舉行時，飯店房價可能會漲到四倍之多。

延伸字 fourfold

● **recreational**

[ˌrɛkrɪ`eʃənl]

(adj.) 消遣的，娛樂的

One of the most interesting ways of enjoying Arizona's fascinating outdoors is in a **recreational** vehicle.

開休旅車旅遊是享受亞利桑那州戶外活動最有趣的方式之一。

延伸字 sporting

refund

[`ri͵fʌnd]

(v.) (n.) 償還，退款

The angry customer demands to see the manager regarding a **refund**.

氣憤的客人要求和經理談有關退款的事情。

延伸字 compensation, settlement, remuneration

---

register

[`rɛdʒɪstɚ]

(v.) 登記，註冊

Remember to **register** before the last day of this month.

記得要在這個月底前完成登記。

延伸字 record, enroll, enter

---

relaxation

[͵rilæks`eʃən]

(n.) 鬆緩，放鬆

While you're working hard, don't forget the importance of **relaxation**.

努力工作的同時，別忘了適度放鬆的重要性。

延伸字 rest, repose, relief

---

release

[rɪ`lis]

(v.) 鬆開，解放，發佈

The company just **released** a statement, apologizing for their defective product.

公司剛剛發佈了一項針對產品缺失的道歉聲明。

延伸字 free, relieve, dismiss

rental

[`rɛntl]

(adj.) 租賃的

(n.) 租賃

Most of the major car **rental** businesses have outlets at airports in New Jersey.

大部分的大型租車公司在紐澤西州各個機場都設有服務站。

---

reservation

[ˌrɛzəˋveʃən]

(n.) 預定，預約，

　　預留

I made a **reservation** last night by phone. Can you check it for me?

我昨晚有打電話過來預約。你能幫我確認一下嗎？

延伸字 booking, retaining

---

respiratory

[rɪˋspaɪrəˌtorɪ]

(adj.) 呼吸的

Air pollution caused by vehicle emissions can be a problem for people with **respiratory** problems.

車輛排放廢氣所造成的空氣污染，對有呼吸道問題的人來說是個困擾。

延伸字 inhaling, panting

---

secretarial

[ˌsɛkrəˋtɛrɪəl]

(adj.) 秘書的，

　　書記的

Most major hotels have business centers for guests' use, and some also offer **secretarial** services.

大部分的大飯店都有商務中心供客人使用，有些還提供秘書服務。

延伸字 assistant

separately

['sɛpərɪtlɪ]

(adv.) 分隔地，
分別地

She placed each file **separately** into different cabinets.

她將檔案分別放到不同的櫃子裡面。

延伸字 apart

---

session

['sɛʃən]

(n.) 會議，集會

We will be holding a **session** to resolve this matter.

我們將會舉行會議來解決這項問題。

延伸字 conference

---

situation

[ˌsɪtʃʊ`eʃən]

(n.) 處境，情況

They have put me in a very awkward **situation**.

他們讓我陷於一個非常尷尬的處境。

延伸字 circumstances, case, condition

---

sophisticated

[sə`fɪstɪˌketɪd]

(adj.) 複雜的，
精密的

Classical music is usually more **sophisticated** than other styles of music, such as rock and country.

古典音樂相較於其他類型的音樂，像是搖滾和鄉村音樂，其旋律較為精緻複雜。

延伸字 complicated

● **spacious**

[ˋspeʃəs]

(adj.) 寬廣的，廣闊的

Generally, inns are large, with **spacious** public areas and a dining room.

一般來說，客棧式旅館都頗大，並有寬敞的公共區域和餐飲區。

延伸字 roomy, extensive

● **spectacular**

[spɛkˋtækjələ˞]

(adj.) 驚人的，壯觀的

The play's ending is **spectacular**. You must see it sometime.

那場表演的結局實在太壯觀了。你一定要找時間去看。

延伸字 dramatic, sensational

● **supersonic**

[͵supɚˋsɑnɪk]

(adj.) 超音速的

(n.) 超音速

The fighter jet went **supersonic**.

戰鬥機進入了超音速模式。

● **tenant**

[ˋtɛnənt]

(n.) 房客，住戶

The landlord is pleased to find such a good **tenant**.

房東很高興能找到一個這麼好的房客。

延伸字 dweller, occupant, resident

terminal

[ˋtɝmənḷ]

(n.) 航站，總站，末端

The Titan International Airport has three **terminals** and receives the bulk of domestic and international arrivals.

大田國際機場有三個航站接待大量的國內外旅客進出。

延伸字 boundary, terminus

---

timetable

[ˋtaɪmˌtebḷ]

(n.) 時刻表，時間表

I've got a very busy **timetable** this week.

我這週的行程非常繁忙。

延伸字 schedule, list

---

tip

[tɪp]

(n.) 小費

The standard **tip** is 15 percent of the cost of the meal.

標準的小費金額是餐飲價格的百分之十五。

延伸字 bonus, premium

---

transaction

[trænˋzækʃən]

(n.) 交易，辦理，執行

Before we loan you the money, we need to check your **transaction** history.

在我們借你錢之前，我們必須先確認你過去的交易歷程。

延伸字 intercourse, proceeding, dealing

translation
[træns`leʃən]
(n.) 翻譯，譯文，譯本

We needed someone to provide us with **translation**, since most of us don't speak Thai.
由於我們大部分都不會講泰語，因此我們需要有人提供翻譯。
延伸字 transcription, decryption, transcript

---

transportation
[͵trænspɚ`teʃən]
(n.) 運輸，輸送

Guide dogs for the blind are allowed on public **transportation**.
導盲犬可以搭乘大眾交通工具。
延伸字 carriage, conveyance

---

uncertainty
[ʌn`sɝtn̩tɪ]
(n.) 不確定，不可靠

You should do your best instead of worrying about **uncertainties**.
你應該盡你所能，而非一味地擔心不確定的事。
延伸字 doubt, skepticism, ambivalence

---

upscale
[`ʌp͵skel]
(adj.) 高檔的，豪華的

We've decided to move to a more **upscale** neighborhood.
我們決定搬到一個更高級的社區。
延伸字 luxurious

utilize

[`jutḷˌaɪz]

(v.) 利用

He **utilizes** his charm to quickly gain the trust of his clients.

他利用自己的魅力迅速地取得客戶的信任。

延伸字 use, employ, apply

---

valid

[`vælɪd]

(adj.) 有效的，
合法的

Visitors who plan to rent a car must remember to bring along a **valid** driver's license and major credit card.

想租車的遊客，要記得準備有效期限內的駕照和信用卡。

延伸字 effective, proven, legal

---

value

[`vælju]

(n.) 價值，益處

Eating out in California is very reasonable, and even expensive restaurants offer good **value**.

在加州，外食的價格還算合理，即便是昂貴的餐廳也是物超所值。

延伸字 excellence, significance

warning

[ˋwɔrnɪŋ]

(n.) 警告，徵候，前兆

Recent financial problems can be viewed as a **warning** of things to come.

最近的金融問題可以看作是未來即將發生的事情的前兆。

延伸字 advice, sign, alarm

5

行銷策略
Marketing Strategy

How many words do you know?
你知道這些字的意思和用法嗎？

- [ ] allocate
- [ ] depreciation
- [ ] leverage
- [ ] pervasive
- [ ] recession
- [ ] subcontract

advanced

[əd`vænst]

(adj.) 在前面的，
先進的

Our company had just installed the most **advanced** security system.

我們公司剛剛安裝了最先進的保全系統。

延伸字 precocious, early

---

advantage

[əd`væntɪdʒ]

(n.) 優勢，利益，
優點

Of all the similar products currently on the market, our product's **advantage** is its price.

相較於目前市面上其他類似產品，我們產品的優勢在於它的價格。

延伸字 superiority, benefit

---

advertising agency

廣告公司

Our branch hired an **advertising agency** to help with promoting our new product.

我們分店請了一間廣告公司來幫我們宣傳新產品。

延伸字 advertising company,
advertising firm

allocate

[ˋæləˌket]

(v.) 分派，分配

My colleague has been **allocated** to another branch.

我的同事被分配到另一個分行了。

延伸字 designate, assign, distribute

---

ascertain

[ˌæsɚˋten]

(v.) 確定，探查

The police are trying to **ascertain** what really happened.

警察正在嘗試查明事情發生的經過。

延伸字 learn, determine

---

attract

[əˋtrækt]

(v.) 引起注意，吸引

The design of our booth **attracted** many customers.

我們攤位的設計吸引了許多客戶。

延伸字 charm, allure, draw, pull

---

avoid

[əˋvɔɪd]

(v.) 避開，躲開，避免

Have you seen Mark lately? I think he's **avoiding** me.

你最近有見到 Mark 嗎？我覺得他刻意在避開我。

延伸字 evade, escape, elude

ban
[bæn]
(v.) 禁止
(n.) 禁令

The government decided to **ban** the use of marijuana.
政府決定禁止人民使用大麻。
延伸字 prohibit, restrict, limit

---

breakthrough
[ˋbrek͵θru]
(n.) 突破點

The writer had a **breakthrough** on his novel.
這位作家在撰寫小說上出現了突破性的進展。
延伸字 discovery

---

budget
[ˋbʌdʒɪt]
(v.) 編列預算
(n.) 預算

The **budget** is pretty tight this year. We might have to cut a few things.
今年的預算很吃緊。我們可能得刪掉一些東西。
延伸字 allocation, resources, apportion

---

buzzword
[ˋbʌzwɝd]
(n.) 時髦用詞

My mom is having a hard time keeping up with the latest **buzzwords**.
我媽媽跟不太上時下最新的流行用語。
延伸字 jargon

campaign

[kæm`pen]

(n.) 活動

We are running a **campaign** to further promote our new product.

我們將舉辦一場活動來進一步宣傳新產品。

延伸字 activity, run, drive

---

challenge

[`tʃælɪndʒ]

(n.) 挑戰，異議，艱鉅的事

When facing a **challenge**, remember to stay calm and focused.

面對挑戰時，記得保持冷靜及專注。

延伸字 dispute, dare

---

collaboration

[kə͵læbə`reʃən]

(n.) 共同研究，合作

The company produced a new product through **collaboration** with the government.

該公司與政府合作推出了一項新的產品。

延伸字 conjunction, complicity

---

collect

[kə`lɛkt]

(v.) 採集，收集，募集

It's Peter's birthday tomorrow. I'm **collecting** funds from everyone for his surprise party.

明天是 Peter 的生日。我正在向大家募集為他舉辦驚喜派對的資金。

延伸字 gather, accumulate, assemble

MP3
26

commercial
[kə`mɝʃəl]
(n.) 廣告
(adj.) 商業的

In Taiwan, **commercial** areas are often mixed with residential areas.
台灣的商業區通常都和住宅區在一起。

延伸字 mercantile

---

compare
[kəm`pɛr]
(v.) 比較，對照

I always **compare** prices on the market before buying expensive products.
我購買昂貴的產品前，都會先比較一下市場上的價格。

延伸字 match, contrast, measure

---

comparison
[kəm`pærəsn̩]
(n.) 比較，對照

Please allow me to show you a visual **comparison** between two products.
請讓我為您展示兩個產品視覺上的對照。

延伸字 likeness, resemblance, similarity

---

compile
[kəm`paɪl]
(v.) 編輯，蒐集

I have been **compiling** data from around the world since the past week.
自上週開始，我一直在蒐集來自世界各地的資料。

延伸字 gather, collect, assemble

comprehensive

[ˌkɑmprɪ`hɛnsɪv]

(adj.) 廣泛的，
有理解力的

He has **comprehensive** knowledge about East Asian languages.

他對於東亞語言有非常廣泛的知識。

延伸字 expansive, thorough

---

conference

[`kɑnfərəns]

(n.) 會議，討論會

Since it's my first time attending a **conference** call, my boss asks me to observe and learn.

由於這是我第一次參加電話會議，老闆要我在一旁邊看邊學。

延伸字 appointment, interchange,
deliberation

---

consistent

[kən`sɪstənt]

(adj.) 一致的，
協調的

Their beliefs have been **consistent** over the past few years.

他們的信念在過去幾年之間一直是一致的。

延伸字 agreeing, accordant, concordant

---

constitute

[`kɑnstəˌtjut]

(v.) 構成，組成，
設立

A committee was **constituted** for irregular payments.

委員會的成立，是為了調查不正常的付款情形。

延伸字 organize, form, establish

○ **demand**

[dɪˋmænd]

(n.) 需求，要求，
請求

The workers want their employer to meet their **demands**.

員工要求雇主達成他們的要求。

延伸字 requirement, requisition, necessity

○ **demographic**

[ˌdɪməˋgræfɪk]

(adj.) 人口統計學
的

The researcher is looking into the latest **demographic** trends.

研究員正在研究最新的人口統計趨勢資料。

延伸字 population

○ **depreciation**

[dɪˌpriʃɪˋeʃən]

(n.) 價值減低，
折舊，跌價

We do not cover any **depreciation** of our products.

我們不負責產品的任何折舊。

延伸字 reduction, slump, fall

○ **detect**

[dɪˋtɛkt]

(v.) 發現，察覺，
查出

He **detected** that someone has been laundering money recently.

他察覺到最近有人在洗錢。

延伸字 discover, locate, recognize

devastate

[ˋdɛvəsˌtet]

(v.) 毀壞

The hurricane **devastated** the whole country.

那場颶風使全國都遭受到破壞。

延伸字 smash, ravage, waste

---

differentiation

[ˌdɪfəˌrɛnʃɪˋeʃən]

(n.) 區別，變異

You really need to learn the **differentiation** between a lion and a tiger.

你真的需要學會分辨獅子和老虎的不同。

延伸字 selection, difference

---

disperse

[dɪˋspɝs]

(v.) 傳播，散發

We are asked to **disperse** pamphlets around the block.

我們被要求在這街區附近發放傳單。

延伸字 scatter, distribute, spread

---

disseminate

[dɪˋsɛməˌnet]

(v.) 散播，宣傳

The newspaper is still a very great way to **disseminate** news.

報紙仍然是一個傳播新聞的好方法。

延伸字 air

● **diversify**

[daɪˋvɝsəˌfaɪ]

(v.) 多樣化

We always think a **diversified** working environment is good for the workers.

我們始終認為多樣化的工作環境對於員工是有幫助的。

延伸字 expand, mix, vary

● **documentary**

[ˌdɑkjəˋmɛntərɪ]

(n.) 文獻

(adj.) 記錄的

I've heard that they are filming a **documentary** on the company's history.

我聽說他們準備要拍一部有關公司歷史沿革的記錄片。

延伸字 narrative, feature, film

● **dominate**

[ˋdɑməˌnet]

(v.) 支配，佔優勢

The market was **dominated** by their company during the past few years.

市場在過去幾年都被他們公司所壟斷。

延伸字 influence, control, overshadow

dynamic
[daɪ`næmɪk]
(adj.) 有生氣的，
　　　蓬勃的

The traditional market in Taiwan is a very **dynamic** place.
台灣的傳統市場是一個非常富有生氣的地方。

延伸字 energetic, lively

---

embrace
[ɪm`bres]
(v.) 擁抱，環繞，
　　　包含

The woman **embraced** her grandson as soon as she opened the door.
那位女士一打開門之後，便將她的孫子抱住。

延伸字 hug, surround, involve

---

expand
[ɪk`spænd]
(v.) 展開，擴大，
　　　發展

Due to the overwhelming success of our last product, the company decides to **expand** its market.
由於我們上一個產品獲得壓倒性的成功，公司決定要擴大其市場。

延伸字 spread, swell, extend

---

experiment
[ɪk`spɛrəmənt]
(n.) 實驗
(v.) 進行試驗

Before we could be sure, let's **experiment** on this first.
在我們可以確定之前，應該先實驗一下。

延伸字 verify, prove, test

extensive
[ɪkˋstɛnsɪv]
(adj.) 多方面的，
廣泛的

For a homemaker, her hobbies are quite **extensive**.

以一個家庭主婦來說，她的興趣還蠻廣泛的。

延伸字 considerable, widespread, boundless

---

eye-catcher
[ˋaɪˌkætʃɚ]
(n.) 引人注目的人
（物）

No matter where she is, her elegance always makes her an **eye-catcher**.

不論身在何處，她的優雅都使她成為引人注目的焦點。

---

fad
[fæd]
(n.) 流行

My wife is always interested in the latest **fads**.

我太太總是對最新的流行很感興趣。

延伸字 fashion, vogue, style, craze

---

finding
[ˋfaɪndɪŋ]
(n.) 調查結果，
發現

I did some research into the company's background, and the **finding** isn't great.

我對該公司的背景做了一些調查，結果並不是很好。

延伸字 discovery, conclusion

foreign

[`fɔrɪn]

(adj.) 外國的，
陌生的

During my trip to Vietnam, everything felt both **foreign** yet familiar.

在越南的旅行途中，我對所有一切都感到既陌生又熟悉。

延伸字 alien, external, outlandish

---

function

[`fʌŋkʃən]

(n.) 功能，作用
(v.) 運作

Each part in a machine serves a **function**.

機器內的每一個零件都各有其功能。

延伸字 work, operate, perform

---

housekeeper

[`haʊsˌkipɚ]

(n.) 家庭主婦，
管家

The **housekeeper** was accused of stealing.

該名管家被指控偷竊。

延伸字 homemaker

---

influx

[`ɪnflʌks]

(n.) 湧進，匯集，
流入

There is a sudden **influx** of refugees due to the civil war across the border.

由於鄰國內戰的因素，突然有非常多的難民湧進我國。

延伸字 inflow

inspect

[ɪn`spɛkt]

(v.) 檢查，審查

I've heard Alice is very strict, and she **inspects** everything in detail.

我聽說 Alice 非常的嚴格，她對所有東西的檢查都非常仔細。

延伸字 examine, observe, study

---

investigate

[ɪn`vɛstə‚get]

(v.) 調查，研究

John was asked to **investigate** the undeveloped market.

John 被派去調查尚未開發的市場。

延伸字 search, explore, research, examine

---

investigation

[ɪn‚vɛstə`geʃən]

(n.) 調查，審查，研究

Facing the incident, the director decides to call for an **investigation**.

面對此一事件，總監決定啟動調查。

延伸字 examination, observation, inspection

---

isolate

[`aɪsl‚et]

(v.) 使隔離，孤立

After he got fired, he **isolated** himself from the world.

在被革職之後，他完全與世隔絕。

延伸字 separate, segregate, disconnect

leading-edge

[`lidɪŋ`ɛdʒ]

(adj.) 最先進的，
高科技的

We have just implemented several **leading-edge** machines.

我們剛剛設置了數台最先進的機器。

延伸字 cutting-edge, state-of-the-art

---

lean

[lin]

(v.) 倚靠，仰賴，
傾斜

We **leaned** against each other while watching the stars.

我們一邊倚靠著彼此，一邊看著星星。

延伸字 bend, slope, incline

---

leverage

[`lɛvərɪdʒ]

(n.) 槓桿作用，
手段，力量

He used the low price as **leverage** to acquire more customers.

他利用低價為手段來爭取更多的客戶。

延伸字 method, power

---

manipulate

[mə`nɪpjə‚let]

(v.) 操作，操控

He tried to **manipulate** me into thinking it's all my fault.

他試著操控我，讓我覺得一切都是我的錯。

延伸字 control

maturity

[məˋtjʊrətɪ]

(n.) 成熟，成熟期

Don't act like a baby and show some **maturity**.

別像個小孩一樣，成熟一點。

延伸字 experience, completion, development

---

media

[ˋmidɪə]

(n.) 媒體

The **media** is a double-edged sword.

媒體是一把雙面刃。

延伸字 news, communications

---

minimize

[ˋmɪnəˏmaɪz]

(v.) 使減到最少，使縮到最小

We must think of a solution quickly to **minimize** the damage.

我們必須盡快想出解決的辦法，使傷害降到最低。

延伸字 lessen, minify, reduce

---

patent

[ˋpætnt]

(n.) 專利權

(v.) 申請專利

This new design was just **patented** last month.

這項新設計在上個月才剛獲得專利。

延伸字 protection, concession

penetrate
[`pɛnə‚tret]
(v.) 滲透，滲入，
打進

The water has **penetrated** the wall and into our house.
水已經滲入牆壁，進到了我們的房子裡。
延伸字 drill, go through, insert

---

penetration
[‚pɛnə`treʃən]
(n.) 滲透，侵入，
穿透力

The **penetration** of that noise is too strong. I can't take it anymore.
那噪音的穿透力實在太強了。我受不了了。
延伸字 entrance, insight

---

perception
[pɚ`sɛpʃən]
(n.) 感知，領悟，
知覺

Some people's **perception** becomes really bad in these tunnels.
有些人在這些隧道裡面時，感官會變得非常遲鈍。
延伸字 awareness, understanding

---

pervasive
[pɚ`vesɪv]
(adj.) 遍佈的，
充斥的

That particular brand is very **pervasive** out there.
那個特定的品牌在外頭非常普遍。
延伸字 widespread

---

practice

[`præktɪs]

(n.) (v.) 練習，
　　　　實行

Don't feel down. Remember that **practice** makes perfect.

別灰心，要記得「熟能生巧」這句話。

延伸字 repeat, train, exercise

---

preparation

[ˌprɛpə`reʃən]

(n.) 準備，預備

The **preparation** of the New Year's feast took hours to complete.

新年大餐的準備，花了數個小時才完成。

延伸字 provision, arrangement, plan

---

priority

[praɪ`ɔrətɪ]

(n.) 優先權，
　　　優先順序

The **priority** of this task is to discover the customers' need.

這項工作的優先目標是去發掘客戶的需求。

延伸字 preference, superiority, order

---

proclaim

[prə`klem]

(v.) 宣佈，聲明

The president **proclaimed** that he will be stepping down next month.

總裁發表聲明，表示他將在下個月退休。

延伸字 declare, announce

---

prohibit

[prə`hɪbɪt]

(v.) 禁止，妨礙，阻止

Smoking is **prohibited** in this building.

這棟大樓內禁止吸菸。

延伸字 forbid, ban, disallow

---

promotion

[prə`moʃən]

(n.) 推廣，升遷

Our manager is retiring in a few months, which means one of us is up for a **promotion**.

我們經理再幾個月就要退休了，這代表我們之中有人可以準備升遷了。

延伸字 advertising, advancement, improvement

---

propaganda

[͵prɑpə`gændə]

(n.) 宣傳活動

Don't trust in their words. It's all **propaganda**.

別相信他們的話，那全都是宣傳而已。

延伸字 advertising, promotion

---

propagate

[`prɑpə͵get]

(v.) 宣傳，增殖

We are trying to **propagate** more interest by showing advertisements on TV.

我們試著藉由電視廣告的播出來增加更多關注。

延伸字 generate, produce, multiply

- **proposal**

  [prə`pozl]

  (n.) 提議，提案，求婚

  I've decided to show my **proposal** directly to the boss.

  我決定直接向老闆提出我的提案。

  延伸字 proposition, recommendation

- **provision**

  [prə`vɪʒən]

  (n.) 供給，預備，儲備

  We should stock up on **provisions** because of the approaching typhoon.

  颱風快來了，我們應該儲備一些補給品。

  延伸字 arrangement, preparation, foundation

- **public relations**

  公共關係

  When a released product is defective, it's up to the **public relations** specialists to minimize the damage.

  當銷售的產品出現問題時，公關部門的專家就必須試圖降低損害。

  延伸字 PR

- **publicity**

  [pʌb`lɪsətɪ]

  (n.) 宣傳

  There is no such thing as bad **publicity**.

  世上沒有所謂的負面宣傳。

  延伸字 announcement, advertising, distribution

● **ratio**

[`reʃo]

(n.) 比例，比率

I got the **ratio** wrong, so I guess the cake is ruined.

我的比例算錯了，所以那個蛋糕大概失敗了。

延伸字 proportion, correlation, rate

● **recession**

[rɪ`sɛʃən]

(n.) 經濟不景氣，衰退

With the **recession** going on, people are much more worried about losing their jobs.

由於經濟不景氣不斷持續，人們越來越擔心會面臨失業問題。

延伸字 decline, inflation

● **reinforce**

[ˌriɪn`fɔrs]

(v.) 增援，加強，強化

The headquarters sent us here to **reinforce** you guys.

總部派我們來這裡支援你們。

延伸字 fortify, strengthen

● **resource**

[rɪ`sors]

(n.) 資源，物力，財力

Each company must manage its **resources** with care.

每間公司皆必須妥善管理其資源。

延伸字 property, goods, possessions, wealth

MP3
30

● **responsibility**

[rɪˌspɑnsəˋbɪlətɪ]

(n.) 責任，責任感

As a teacher, you must have a **responsibility** towards your students.

為人師長，就必須對學生有責任感。

延伸字 duty, obligation, burden

● **segment**

[ˋsɛgmənt]

(n.) 部分

In this **segment** of the show, we will be showing some magic tricks.

我們在這段節目中，將會表演魔術秀。

延伸字 division, section, part

● **separate**

[ˋsɛpəˌret]

(v.) 分割

The product line was **separated** into two.

該產品線被一分為二。

延伸字 split

● **significant**

[sɪgˋnɪfəkənt]

(adj.) 顯著的，
重大的

It's an individual incident, which is not **significant** enough to impact our strategy.

那只是一個獨立事件，還沒有嚴重到足以影響我們的策略。

延伸字 important, considerable,
substantial

slogan

[`slogən]

(n.) 標語，口號

If we want this campaign to work, we need to find a good **slogan** first.

如果這場活動要成功的話，我們必須先想出一個好口號才行。

延伸字 expression, phrase, saying

---

spectrum

[`spɛktrəm]

(n.) 譜，光譜，幅度

The primary colors of the **spectrum** are red, yellow and blue.

光譜的原色為紅、黃與藍。

延伸字 range, hue cycle, series

---

spokesman

[`spoksmən]

(n.) 發言人，代言人

The **spokesman** assures the press that no one got hurt.

發言人向媒體保證沒有人受傷。

延伸字 representative, delegate, mediator

---

spread

[sprɛd]

(v.) 擴散

The flu **spread** very quickly around my office.

感冒在我的辦公室內很快地擴散開來了。

延伸字 disperse, scatter

○ **strategy**

[`strætədʒɪ]

(n.) 策略

Our product **strategy** is to play the "budget" card.

我們的產品策略是打「低價」牌。

延伸字 planning, approach, tactics

○ **subcontract**

[sʌb`kɑntrækt]

(v.) 轉包

Our manager **subcontracted** some of the work to an outside source.

我們經理將部分工作轉包給公司以外的人員。

延伸字 farm out

○ **survey**

[sɚ`ve]

(n.) 調查

A customer **survey** is a great source of information.

客戶問卷調查是很好的資訊來源。

延伸字 inspection

○ **target audience**

目標客戶群

For this tour, our **target audience** will be blue-collar workers.

這次行程的目標族群是藍領階級的勞工。

延伸字 target market

theme

[θim]

(n.) 論題，話題，主題

The **theme** for our promotion should be focused on the upcoming holiday.

我們促銷活動的主題，應該著重在即將到來的節日。

延伸字 subject, topic, text

---

ultimate

[ˋʌltəmɪt]

(adj.) 最後的，最終的

Acquiring equal rights is the **ultimate** goal of the meeting.

獲得平等權利是這場會議的最終目標。

延伸字 last, final, terminal

---

unique selling point

賣點

You need to find a **unique selling point** for your product first.

你需要先找出自己產品的賣點。

延伸字 USP

---

usury

[ˋjuʒʊrɪ]

(n.) 高利貸

Before borrowing money from loan sharks, it's best to be familiar with the **usury** laws.

向地下錢莊借錢之前，最好先熟悉一下高利貸的相關法律。

延伸字 exploitation

▶ variety

[vəˋraɪətɪ]

(n.) 多樣性，變化

Our company offers a **variety** of solutions to help you with your problem.

本公司提供許多不同的解決方案，來協助您解決問題。

延伸字 difference, diversity, variation

▶ word-of-mouth

[ˋwɝdəvˋmaʊθ]

(adj.) 口耳相傳的

Word-of-mouth marketing through social media sites has proven very effective.

經由社群網站進行口碑式行銷，已被證明是非常有效的方式。

延伸字 oral communication, viva-voce

6

業務銷售

Sales Performance

How many words do you know?
你知道這些字的意思和用法嗎？

- [ ] benchmark
- [ ] commodity
- [ ] dividend
- [ ] fluctuate
- [ ] ledger
- [ ] unprecedented

accessible

[æk`sɛsəbl̩]

(adj.) 可得到的，
可使用的

Don't worry, their service is very **accessible**.

別擔心，他們的服務非常便民。

延伸字 approachable, affable, obtainable

---

appropriate

[ə`proprɪˌet]

(adj.) 適當的，
恰當的

Please forward this letter to the **appropriate** sales representative.

請將此信轉給負責的業務代表。

延伸字 suitable, fitting, proper

---

auction

[`ɔkʃən]

(n.) (v.) 拍賣

I bought this antique vase from an **auction**.

我在一場拍賣會上買了這個古董花瓶。

延伸字 bargain

---

balance

[`bæləns]

(n.) 平衡

(v.) 結算，抵消

It's important to keep a good **balance** between work and private life.

保持工作與私人生活之間的平衡是非常重要的。

延伸字 compensate, correspond,
counteract

bargain

[ˋbɑrgɪn]

(n.) 協議，協定，
交易

This is looking more and more like a losing **bargain**.

這看起來越來越像是一項虧本的交易。

延伸字 agreement, contract

---

battle

[ˋbætl̩]

(n.) 戰鬥，戰役，
鬥爭

Get ready, because there will be a hard **battle** ahead.

準備好，一場艱困的戰鬥即將到來。

延伸字 encounter, disagreement, hostility

---

benchmark

[ˋbɛntʃˏmɑrk]

(n.) 水準點，基準

His performance is so good that we all use his track record as a **benchmark**.

他的表現好到我們都用他的業績來當基準。

延伸字 criterion

---

benefit

[ˋbɛnəfɪt]

(n.) 利益，優勢

(v.) 有益於，受惠

Before learning the whole story, it's best to give the person involved the **benefit** of the doubt.

在了解事情的全貌之前，最好先假定當事人是無辜的。

延伸字 bestead, advantage, profit

burden

[ˋbɝˋdn̩]

(n.) 負荷，義務，
重擔

The financial **burden** will be more evenly shared.

資金的負擔將會更平均地分攤。

延伸字 load, charge, task

---

capacity

[kəˋpæsətɪ]

(n.) 容量，容積

The hard drive usage is nearing its maximum **capacity**.

硬碟的使用量已經接近它的最大容量了。

延伸字 size, volume, content

---

catalog

[ˋkætəlɔg]

(n.) 目錄，目錄冊

Our client asked to see the product **catalog** first, before making any decisions.

我們的客戶要求在做決定之前，先看一下產品的目錄。

延伸字 file

---

ceiling

[ˋsilɪŋ]

(n.) 天花板，
最高限額

The **ceiling** at my place is leaking. I had better call the landlord.

我住處的天花板在漏水。我最好趕快打電話給房東。

延伸字 top, record, superiority

circumstance

[`sɝkəm͵stæns]

(n.) 情況，環境，情勢

You should not lend him money under any **circumstances**.

不管在什麼情況之下都不能借錢給他。

延伸字 condition, situation, state

---

collaborate

[kə`læbə͵ret]

(v.) 合作，協同，合夥

We have **collaborated** with several partners in order to bring you this fine product.

我們和數名合作夥伴協力為您帶來這份精美的產品。

延伸字 cooperate, participate, join forces

---

commodity

[kə`madətɪ]

(n.) 商品，日用品

The merchant brought several **commodities** to the small village.

商人將好幾種商品帶到了小村落中。

延伸字 product, ware

---

condition

[kən`dɪʃən]

(n.) 條件

Before I agree to this, I have a few **conditions** myself.

在我同意之前，我自己也有幾項條件。

延伸字 provision, specification

confidential

[ˌkɑnfəˋdɛnʃəl]

(adj.) 機密的

The content in that package is strictly **confidential**.

那件包裹裡面裝的東西是絕對機密的。

延伸字 secret, off the record

---

convention

[kənˋvɛnʃən]

(n.) 會議，集會，
展覽會

Are you also in town for the big **convention**?

你來這座城市也是為了參加那場大型會議嗎？

延伸字 exhibition, trade show

---

convey

[kənˋve]

(v.) 運送，搬運，
傳遞

I'm having a hard time **conveying** my thoughts.

我傳達不太出來我的想法。

延伸字 carry, transport, deliver

---

convince

[kənˋvɪns]

(v.) 使確定，
使信服

He tried to **convince** me he has changed, but I remain skeptical.

他試著說服我他已經改變了，但我仍然抱持懷疑的態度。

延伸字 persuade, assure, promise

coordinator

[koˋɔrdn͵etɚ]

(n.) 協調者，
同等的人

Coordinators are important between two parties.

兩方之間的協調者扮演了很重要的角色。

延伸字 administrator, organizer

---

counselor

[ˋkaʊnslɚ]

(n.) 顧問

I need a credit counselor to help with my current financial goals.

我需要一位信貸顧問來協助完成我當前的財務目標。

延伸字 advisor, guide, coach

---

covet

[ˋkʌvɪt]

(v.) 妄想，垂涎

He has been coveting that position for years.

他已經垂涎那個職位好幾年了。

延伸字 want, envy

---

currency

[ˋkɝənsɪ]

(n.) 通貨，貨幣

The Pacific country Niue shares the same currency as New Zealand.

位於太平洋的國家紐埃使用與紐西蘭一樣的貨幣。

延伸字 money, cash

debt

[dɛt]

(n.) 債，借款

Thank you for helping me today. I am in your **debt**.

今天感謝你的幫忙。我欠你一份情。

延伸字 obligation, amount due

---

declining

[dɪ`klaɪnɪŋ]

(adj.) 日漸衰退的

Our business has been **declining** ever since the financial crisis.

自從金融危機之後，我們的生意就開始日漸衰退。

延伸字 weakening

---

defective

[dɪ`fɛktɪv]

(adj.) 缺陷的，
　　　不完美的

Can we replace this **defective** machine with a new one?

我們可以要求將這部有問題的機器換新嗎？

延伸字 imperfect, deficient, faulty

---

deficit

[`dɛfɪsɪt]

(n.) 赤字，不足額

The CEO took all the responsibility for the **deficit**.

執行長扛下造成赤字的所有責任。

延伸字 shortfall, shortage, deficiency

delivery

[dɪˋlɪvərɪ]

(n.) 遞送（貨）

I think I've heard some noise. It must be the pizza **delivery** man.

我好像聽到一些聲音，一定是外送比薩的人。

延伸字 transference

---

deserve

[dɪˋzɜˑv]

(v.) 應得，應受

After 5 years, Kate finally got promoted. She **deserved** it.

Kate 在五年之後終於晉升了。這是她應得的。

延伸字 warrant, earn, gain

---

designate

[ˋdɛzɪɡ͵net]

(v.) 指出，指定

Wayne was **designated** to lead the new team.

Wayne 被指派去帶領新團隊。

延伸字 show, indicate, specify

---

dimension

[dɪˋmɛnʃən]

(n.) 尺寸，容積，次元

The factory worker was asked to measure the precise **dimension** of the package.

工廠的員工被要求對該包裹的尺寸進行精確的測量。

延伸字 magnitude, proportion, capacity

distribute
[dɪ`strɪbjʊt]
(v.) 分發，分配，
分開

Kenny wants me to help him **distribute** the healthcare pamphlets.
Kenny 要我幫他分發醫療保健簡章。
延伸字 scatter, spread, dispense

---

divide
[də`vaɪd]
(v.) 使分開，劃分

A river **divides** the field into two parts.
一條河將那塊土地分成兩半。
延伸字 separate, portion, partition

---

dividend
[`dɪvəˌdɛnd]
(n.) 股利，股息

We've all received a large sum of **dividends** last year.
我們去年都獲得了一大筆股息。
延伸字 surplus, interest, portion

---

downturn
[`daʊntɝn]
(n.) 下跌，沉滯

The economy took a **downturn** right after the stock market crash.
在股災發生之後，經濟便迅速地開始衰退。
延伸字 decline, plunge, slump

durable

[ˋdjʊrəbḷ]

(adj.) 經久的，耐用的

If it's really up to me, I would choose the one that is more **durable**.

如果真的要我決定的話，我會選比較耐用的那一個。

延伸字 enduring, permanent, sturdy, solid

---

dwindling

[ˋdwɪndlɪŋ]

(adj.) 日漸減少的

The **dwindling** rate of birth is very alarming.

日漸減少的出生率，令人非常擔憂。

延伸字 lessening, diminishing

---

element

[ˋɛləmənt]

(n.) 要素，成分

We need the **element** of surprise to gain advantage over our competitor.

我們需要出其不意才能在競爭上取得優勢。

延伸字 component, constituent, ingredient

---

endangered

[ɪnˋdendʒɚd]

(adj.) 受到威脅的

The company was **endangered** by the financial crisis.

金融危機對該公司造成了威脅。

延伸字 threatened

> **enormity**
> [ɪˋnɔrmətɪ]
> (n.) 龐大，巨大

The **enormity** of the challenge is unimaginable.
這個挑戰的巨大程度是我們根本想像不到的。

延伸字 greatness, vastness

> **equipment**
> [ɪˋkwɪpmənt]
> (n.) 設備，裝備

Please be gentle. That is new **equipment**.
請小心點，那可是新設備。

延伸字 apparatus, gear, appointments

> **equivalent**
> [ɪˋkwɪvələnt]
> (n.) 相等物
> (adj.) 相等的

One inch is **equivalent** to 2.54 centimeters.
1 英吋等於 2.54 公分。

延伸字 equal, match, rival

> **estimate**
> [ˋɛstəˌmet]
> (v.) 估計，估量，
>   評價

Our team of experts **estimates** that the stock price would go down 1%.
我們的專業團隊估計股價將會下跌 1%。

延伸字 judge, calculate, evaluate

eventually

[ɪˋvɛntʃʊəlɪ]

(adv.) 最終

I knew you would change your mind **eventually**.

我知道你最終一定會改變想法的。

延伸字 finally, ultimately

---

examine

[ɪgˋzæmɪn]

(v.) 檢查，細查，分析

The doctor **examined** the patient carefully.

醫生很仔細地檢查了病患。

延伸字 inspect, observe, study

---

exclusive

[ɪkˋsklusɪv]

(adj.) 排外的，獨家的

We own the **exclusive** right to sell this product.

我們擁有這項產品的獨家銷售權。

延伸字 sole, entire, incompatible

---

expense

[ɪkˋspɛns]

(n.) 花費，開支，費用

My manager is very strict on my business **expense**.

我的主管對我業務上的開銷管得非常嚴格。

延伸字 expenditure, outlay

expertise

[ˌɛkspɚˋtiz]

(n.) 專門技術，
專家意見

They recruited me because I have the **expertise** they need.

由於我擁有他們需要的專門技術，他們雇用了我。

延伸字 competence, expertness, proficiency

---

fluctuate

[ˋflʌktʃʊˌet]

(v.) 波動，變化

The price of gold **fluctuated** widely last month.

上個月金價大幅波動。

延伸字 wave, swing, shift

---

generate

[ˋdʒɛnəˌret]

(v.) 產生，發生，
引起

We spent a lot of money on advertisements to **generate** interest in new products.

為了引起大家對新產品的興趣，我們花了很多錢在廣告上。

延伸字 produce, cause, create

- **greenback**

  [ˈgrinˌbæk]

  (n.) 美鈔

  Buying **greenbacks** as an investment is not a bad idea.

  購買美鈔做為投資不算是個壞主意。

  延伸字 currency, money, bill

- **haggle**

  [ˈhægl]

  (v.) 爭論不休，
  討價還價

  He preferred to be overcharged than to **haggle**.

  他寧願支付過多的金額，也不願意討價還價。

  延伸字 truck, bargain

- **hoard**

  [hord]

  (v.) 囤積，窖藏，
  私藏

  It is wrong to **hoard** up on essential goods and sell them for a higher price.

  囤積民生必需品並用更高的價格轉賣，是不對的行為。

  延伸字 accumulate, collect, cache

- **indicator**

  [ˈɪndəˌketɚ]

  (n.) 顯示，指標

  The GM's visit is a clear **indicator** of the two companies' growing relationship.

  總經理的造訪很明確地顯示出，兩家公司的關係已越走越近。

  延伸字 show, exhibit, demonstrate

● **inflation**
[ɪnˋfleʃən]
(n.) 通貨膨脹，
　　充氣，膨脹

Inflation is inevitable; just look at how much 100 dollars was worth 50 years ago.
通貨膨脹是必然的，只要看看 100 元在 50 年前的價值是多少就好。

延伸字 boost, rise, spread

● **instrument**
[ˋɪnstrəmənt]
(n.) 儀器，器具，
　　機械

Please be careful. These **instruments** are all very fragile.
請小心，這些儀器都非常容易損壞。

延伸字 tool, device, utensil

● **intact**
[ɪnˋtækt]
(adj.) 原封不動，
　　完整無缺的

He promised to return it to me **intact**.
他保證會將它原封不動地還給我。

延伸字 untouched, undamaged, pristine

● **intangible**
[ɪnˋtændʒəbl]
(adj.) 無形的，
　　不可觸摸的

Somehow I got an **intangible** feeling that someone's watching me.
不知為何我有種莫名的感覺，好像有人在看著我一般。

延伸字 untouchable, unsubstantial

inventory

[ˈɪnvənˌtorɪ]

(n.) 存貨清單，
詳細目錄

The manager asks me to stay and check the **inventory**.

經理要我留下來檢查存貨清單。

延伸字 summary, stock, catalog

---

investor

[ɪnˈvɛstɚ]

(n.) 投資人

My father believed in me and my company, and became its first **investor**.

我父親相信我和我的公司，並成為公司的第一位投資人。

延伸字 investment

---

launch

[lɔntʃ]

(v.) 發起，開始

Our new product **launched** with extreme success.

我們的新產品一發售即相當成功。

延伸字 start, introduce, spring

---

layout

[ˈleˌaʊt]

(n.) 安排，設計，
佈局

The **layout** of the office is quite inconvenient.

這間辦公室的空間設計蠻不方便的。

延伸字 construction, formation

● **lease**
[lis]
(v.) 出租，租

The lady decided to **lease** out her apartment.
那位女士決定將她的公寓出租。

延伸字 rent, hire, let, charter

● **ledger**
[ˈlɛdʒɚ]
(n.) 底帳，總帳

Our accountant found several inconsistencies in the **ledger**.
我們的會計在總帳內找到數個不一致的地方。

延伸字 journal, account book

● **legitimacy**
[lɪˈdʒɪtəməsɪ]
(n.) 適當，正當，合法性

You have to submit further proof of the **legitimacy** of this document.
你必須提出進一步證明這份文件合法性的證據。

延伸字 authority, validity, right

lucrative

[ˈlukrətɪv]

(adj.) 賺錢的，
　　　有獲利的

He currently owns a **lucrative** business downtown.

他目前在市中心擁有一家生意還不錯的公司。

延伸字 moneymaking, remunerative, profitable

---

margin

[ˈmardʒɪn]

(n.) 邊緣，餘裕，
　　邊界空白處

This price will make a reasonable profit **margin**.

這個價格可以有不錯的獲利空間。

延伸字 edge, gross profit, surplus

---

marketplace

[ˈmarkɪtˌples]

(n.) 商業中心，
　　市場

I always go to the morning **marketplace** on Saturday morning.

我總是在星期六早上去早市。

延伸字 mart, outlet

---

massive

[ˈmæsɪv]

(adj.) 厚重的，
　　　巨大的

That thing is **massive**; there's no way I can lift it up by myself.

那東西太大了，我不可能一個人把它抬起來。

延伸字 big, large

● **material**
[məˋtɪrɪəl]
(n.) 資料，素材

We urge you to look over the enclosed **materials** and consider this special offer now.

我們建議您參考附上的資料，可立即享有此優惠。

延伸字 substance, stuff

● **merchant**
[ˋmɝtʃənt]
(n.) 商人，店主

The **merchant** offered me a cash discount.

那位商人提供我現金的折扣。

延伸字 vendor

● **multitasking**
[ˌmʌltɪˋtæskɪŋ]
(n.) 多重作業，
多重任務

I am great at **multitasking**; I can answer the phone while typing out reports.

我很會一心多用，我能一邊講電話一邊打報告。

● **navigate**
[ˋnævəˌget]
(v.) 操縱，導航，
飛行

I am new to this city, and having a hard time **navigating** around.

我才剛來這座城市，所以還不太認得路。

延伸字 guide, cruise, steer

negotiate

[nɪˋgoʃɪˌet]

(v.) 商議，談判，
交涉

My colleague tried very hard to **negotiate** a better price, but eventually he failed.

我的同事很努力地嘗試商議更好的價格，但最後還是失敗了。

延伸字 adjudicate

---

obligation

[ˌabləˋgeʃən]

(n.) 義務，責任

There is absolutely no cost or **obligation** on your part.

您這部分絕不需支付任何費用或負擔任何義務。

延伸字 requirement, compulsion, demand

---

overwhelming

[ˌovɚˋhwɛlmɪŋ]

(adj.) 壓倒性的，
大受打擊的

He is really stressed out with the **overwhelming** number of cases.

壓倒性的大量案件，使他感到沉重的壓力。

延伸字 staggering, stunning

---

packaging

[ˋpækɪdʒɪŋ]

(n.) 包裝

The **packaging** of my parcel is bad. My goods are damaged because of it.

由於這個包裹的包裝很糟糕，我的商品因而受到損壞。

延伸字 wrapping

○ **performance**
[pə`fɔrməns]
(n.) 執行，表演，
效能

We are all very pleased with the new photocopier's **performance**.
我們全都對新影印機的效能感到很滿意。
延伸字 representation, interpretation, effectiveness

○ **plunge**
[plʌndʒ]
(v.) 跌落，下滑，
陷入

The cat **plunged** down the tree after hearing his owner.
聽到主人的聲音之後，那隻貓便從樹上衝了下來。
延伸字 descend, plummet, dive

○ **predict**
[prɪ`dɪkt]
(v.) 預期，預測

People can never **predict** what would happen next.
沒有人可以預測接下來會發生的事。
延伸字 foresee

presentation

[ˌprizɛnˈteʃən]

(n.) 上演，演出

The **presentation** will start at 9 o'clock, and we will rehearse before 8.

演出將在九點開始，而我們將在八點前排練。

延伸字 performance, expression

---

proliferate

[prəˈlɪfəˌret]

(v.) 激增，擴散，增殖

The bacteria **proliferated** with immense speed.

細菌以驚人的速度增殖了。

延伸字 reproduce, generate, multiply

---

prosper

[ˈprɑspɚ]

(v.) 昌盛，繁榮，成功

The company started to **prosper** three years after its establishment.

公司在成立三年之後，生意開始興隆了起來。

延伸字 flourish, advance, benefit

---

provision

[prəˈvɪʒən]

(n.) 供應，提供，裝備

Before we set out camping, it's best to recheck our **provisions**.

我們出發去露營之前，最好重新檢查一遍我們的裝備。

延伸字 supply, providing, outfitting

provoke

[prə`vok]

(v.) 激起，誘導，
挑釁

He's really angry already; try not to **provoke** him.

他已經很生氣了，試著別去激怒他。

延伸字 stir, excite, irritate

---

radical

[`rædɪkl]

(adj.) 根本的，
基本的

We must find the **radical** cause of this problem.

我們必須找出這項問題的根本原因。

延伸字 base, fundamental

---

receivable

[rɪ`sivəbl]

(adj.) 可接受的，
可承認的

I found your terms **receivable**, and would like to discuss further.

我可以接受您的條件，並且想進一步做討論。

延伸字 acceptable

---

recovery

[rɪ`kʌvərɪ]

(n.) 復原，恢復，
痊癒

Jake is still in **recovery** from that car crash.

Jake 在那場車禍所受的傷仍然在復原當中。

延伸字 restoration, improvement, replacement

rectify

[ˋrɛktəˌfaɪ]

(v.) 矯正，調節

I aim to **rectify** this mistake by coming up with a new plan.

我要制定出一項新計劃來修正這個錯誤。

延伸字 adjust, remedy, regulate

---

rehearse

[rɪˋhɝs]

(v.) 排練，排演

In order to give the best performance, we will **rehearse** every night.

為了做出最棒的表演，我們每天晚上都會排練。

延伸字 practice, train

---

replace

[rɪˋples]

(v.) 把…放回，取代，歸還

We are starting to **replace** the old machines with new ones.

我們開始用新機器取代舊機器。

延伸字 substitute for, fill in for

---

reprint

[ˋriˌprɪnt]

(v.) 再印，轉載

I would like your permission to **reprint** some material from your book.

我想請求您的許可，讓我可以轉載您書中的部分內容。

延伸字 reproduction

restore
[rɪˋstor]
(v.) 恢復，重建，
復原

It's going to take a while before the people could **restore** faith.

人們要恢復信心還需要一段時間。

延伸字 strengthen, renovate, reinforce

---

revenue
[ˋrɛvəˌnju]
(n.) 收入

A company must generate **revenue** in order to survive.

一家公司必須要有收入才能夠生存下去。

延伸字 return, gross, income

---

robot
[ˋrobət]
(n.) 自動控制裝置
，機器人

Walking can be difficult even for the most advanced **robot**.

就算是最先進的機器人，走起路來也不是件簡單的事。

延伸字 automation, android, machine

---

roughly
[ˋrʌflɪ]
(adv.) 粗略地，
大概地

I've counted **roughly** 60 people in this plaza.

我粗略計算大概有 60 人在這個廣場上。

延伸字 approximately, more or less

routine

[ruˋtin]

(n.) 例行公事，
慣例

It is her **routine** to arrive 7 minutes early for every meeting.

無論任何會議，她的慣例都是提早七分鐘抵達。

延伸字 procedure, quotidian

---

satisfy

[ˋsætɪsˌfaɪ]

(v.) 使滿意

If you are not completely **satisfied**, simply return it for a full refund.

若您對產品不甚滿意，可以全額退款。

延伸字 please, gratify, benefit

---

shipment

[ˋʃɪpmənt]

(n.) 裝載的貨物，
裝運

We are still waiting for the latest **shipment**; it is already 3 days late.

我們還在等最近的那批貨物，它已經延誤三天了。

延伸字 transport, freight, cargo, load

---

skyrocket

[ˋskaɪˌrɑkɪt]

(v.) 突然攀升，
猛漲

Ever since the product launched, the company's stock price has **skyrocketed**.

自從這項產品發售之後，該公司的股價便一飛衝天。

延伸字 rocket

slash
[slæʃ]
(v.) 大幅刪減，
猛砍

Our budget for this year has been **slashed** in half.

我們今年的預算被砍了一半。

延伸字 chop, abridge, cut down

---

stability
[stə`bɪlətɪ]
(n.) 安定，堅定，
穩定性

Your arrogance is going to harm the **stability** of this company.

你的傲慢將會傷害到這間公司的穩定性。

延伸字 assurance, adherence, endurance

---

standardize
[`stændəd͵aɪz]
(v.) 使標準化，
使統一

We are trying to **standardize** the connectors for these machines.

我們正試著將這些機器的接頭統一。

延伸字 regiment

---

statement
[`stetmənt]
(n.) 陳述，聲明，
財務報告

The reporters asked the senator to give a **statement** regarding the scandal.

記者們要求議員針對醜聞發表聲明。

延伸字 announcement, description, communication

stock

[stɑk]

(n.) (v.) 儲存，存貨

When we finally decided on which model to get, the clerk told us they are out of **stock**.

當我們終於決定好要買的型號，店員卻告訴我們已經沒有存貨了。

延伸字 collect, accumulate, stockpile

---

substantial

[səb`stænʃəl]

(adj.) 大量的，重要的

In order to achieve this, we need a **substantial** amount of money.

想要達成這件事，我們需要巨額的資金才行。

延伸字 wealthy, prosperous, affluent

---

substantially

[səb`stænʃəlɪ]

(adv.) 本質上，相當多地

After a typhoon, the price of fruits and vegetables may go up **substantially**.

颱風過後，蔬菜水果的價格可能會大幅上揚。

延伸字 largely, considerably

---

subtle

[`sʌtl]

(adj.) 敏感的，微妙的

He is very **subtle** when it comes to expressing his feelings.

他在表達感情時會變得非常含蓄。

延伸字 sophisticated, inconspicuous

● **successive**

[səkˋsɛsɪv]

(adj.) 連續的，
系列的

We have had three **successive** years of trade deficit.

我們曾經連續三年都呈現貿易赤字。

延伸字 consecutive, serial, in a row

● **sustainable**

[səˋstenəbl]

(adj.) 可維持的，
足以支撐的

It is very important for humans to find a new **sustainable** energy.

找出一個新的永續能源，對於人類而言是非常重要的。

延伸字 bearable, endurable

● **textile**

[ˋtɛkstaɪl]

(n.) 紡織品，
紡織原料

The workers at the **textile** factory are having a strike.

紡織工廠的員工正在進行罷工。

延伸字 material, cloth, fabric

turnover

[`tɜn͵ovɚ]

(n.) 人員更換率，
營業額，
流通量

Our employees are staying longer;
turnover is decreasing.

我們的員工留任時間變長，流動率降低
了。

We will likely reach a higher **turnover**
during the holiday season.

我們在過節的這段時間，很有可能會達到
更高的營業額。

---

unprecedented

[ʌn`prɛsə͵dɛntɪd]

(adj.) 前所未有的
，空前的

We are making this **unprecedented** offer
to a select group of business executives.

我們提供前所未有的優惠給特選的業務主
管。

延伸字 exceptional, extraordinary

---

vendor

[`vɛndɚ]

(n.) 推銷員，小販

The **vendor** is selling his products at a
discounted price.

那位推銷員用優惠價格在販售他的產品。

延伸字 salesman, peddler, trader

volume
[ˋvɑljəm]
(n.) 體積，量

The work **volume** is pretty okay, no pressure.
工作量還算可以，不會有壓力。

延伸字 amount, quantity, capacity

---

withhold
[wɪðˋhold]
(v.) 保留，隱瞞

Please don't **withhold** any information from us; it is vital to us.
請不要對我們隱瞞任何資訊，它們對我們而言非常重要。

延伸字 reserve, keep, preserve

---

yield
[jild]
(v.) 生產，供給，
提供

Our new store has **yielded** a lot of revenue.
我們的新店面創造了許多收益。

延伸字 produce, give, grant

職場人事
Jobs and Personnel

7

How many words do you know?
你知道這些字的意思和用法嗎？

- [ ] apprentice
- [ ] commensurate
- [ ] inauguration
- [ ] merit
- [ ] reimburse
- [ ] supremacy

absence
[`æbsns]
(n.) 缺乏，缺席，不在場

Matt is currently on a leave of **absence**. Please see Tom instead.

Matt 目前請假中，請改找 Tom。

延伸字 nonattendance, unavailability, lack

---

achievement
[ə`tʃivmənt]
(n.) 成就，完成，達到

One of my greatest **achievements** is having you as my son.

我最大的成就之一，就是能有你這個兒子。

延伸字 accomplishment, fulfillment, consummation

---

administrator
[əd`mɪnəˌstretɚ]
(n.) 行政人員，管理人

The Internet is down again. Somebody go find the system **administrator**.

網路又斷線了，誰快去通知一下系統管理員。

延伸字 executive, director, supervisor

---

affirmative
[ə`fɝmətɪv]
(adj.) 肯定的，保證的

The boss gave an **affirmative** answer to our proposal.

老闆對我們的提案給了肯定的答覆。

延伸字 assertive, positive, emphatic

ambition

[æm`bɪʃən]

(n.) 雄心，抱負，野心

Sarah is a woman with great **ambition**. She became the VP of the company in just 5 years.

Sarah 是一位非常有野心的女性，她在短短五年內成為了公司的副總經理。

延伸字 aspiration, desire, initiative

---

apprentice

[ə`prɛntɪs]

(n.) 徒弟，見習生

He took in an **apprentice** to help with his work.

他找了一位學徒來協助他的工作。

延伸字 amateur, student, learner

---

approachable

[ə`protʃəbl̩]

(adj.) 易接近的，親切的

I like the new manager; he has a really **approachable** personality.

我還蠻喜歡新主管的，他的個性非常平易近人。

延伸字 reachable, attainable, affable

---

aspire

[ə`spaɪr]

(v.) 渴望，追求，有志於

Many of our workers here **aspire** for success.

許多我們的員工都渴望獲得成功。

延伸字 desire, yearn, dream

▶ background
[ˋbæk͵graʊnd]
(n.) 背景，經歷

The new girl has a vast **background** in marketing research.
新來的女生擁有豐富的市場調查背景。

延伸字 experience, knowledge

▶ behavior
[bɪˋhevjɚ]
(n.) 行為舉止，
態度

Is there something wrong with Bruce? His **behavior** this morning is strange.
Bruce 發生什麼事了嗎？他今天早上的行為舉行很奇怪。

延伸字 conduct, action, manner

▶ broker
[ˋbrokɚ]
(n.) 股票（或證
券）經紀人，
中間人

My friend always dreamed of becoming a **broker**.
我的朋友一直想要成為一位證券經紀人。

延伸字 stockbroker, intermediary, agent, mediator

▶ candidate
[ˋkændədet]
(n.) 候選人，
候補者

Gary is a hot **candidate** for the manager position.
Gary 是接任經理職位的熱門人選。

延伸字 nominee, applicant

---

canteen

[kæn`tin]

(n.) 販賣部，
福利社

I'm thirsty. Do you want to get a drink at the **canteen**?

我口渴了。你想去販賣部買個飲料嗎？

延伸字 store

---

carrier

[`kærɪɚ]

(n.) 搬運者，
運送人

Since there's no one home, the **carrier** left a message on the door.

由於沒有人在家，送貨員在門上留了一張字條。

延伸字 transporter, conveyor, messenger

---

claimant

[`klemənt]

(n.) 主張者，
要求者

He was one of the **claimants** to the position.

他是力爭該職位的其中一人。

延伸字 complainant, claimer

---

commensurate

[kə`mɛnʃərɪt]

(adj.) 同量的，
相稱的

We want to make sure we're addressing it in a way that's **commensurate** with the risk.

我們想確保能夠提出與風險相應的解決方法。

延伸字 corresponding, comparable

MP3
40

○ **compatible**
[kəm`pætəbļ]
(adj.) 能共處的，
能並存的

We broke up yesterday; I don't think we are **compatible**.

我們昨天分手了，我不認為我們適合彼此。

延伸字 appropriate, congenial, cooperative

○ **compensation**
[ˌkampən`seʃən]
(n.) 賠償，薪資，
補償金

The customers are asking the store to give them **compensation**.

消費者要求店家給他們賠償。

延伸字 repayment, reimbursement

○ **complimentary**
[ˌkamplə`mɛntərɪ]
(adj.) 恭維的，
讚美的

My boss is very **complimentary** about my work from last month.

我的老闆對於我上個月的工作表現極為稱讚。

延伸字 appreciative, respectful

○ **consolidation**
[kənˌsalə`deʃən]
(n.) 鞏固，團結，
合併

Our team is in dire need of **consolidation** right now.

我們的團隊目前非常急需團結一心。

延伸字 integration, association, unification

courtesy

[`kɝ·təsɪ]

(n.) 謙恭，殷勤，
禮貌

He wrote her a thank-you note out of
courtesy.

出於禮貌，他寫了一張感謝卡給她。

延伸字 politeness, courteousness, respect

---

create

[krɪ`et]

(v.) 創造，創作，
創建

In order to **create** more revenue, we need
to think outside the box.

若要創造更多營收，我們就得發揮更出色
的創意。

延伸字 make, form, invent

---

credential

[krɪ`dɛnʃəl]

(n.) 憑證，證件

The security guard asked us for some
credentials before letting us through.

保全人員要我們先出示證件才能讓我們通
過。

延伸字 certificate, document

---

cubicle

[`kjubɪkl̩]

(n.) 小隔間

Each one of us has a **cubicle** in the office.

我們每個人在辦公室都有一個小隔間。

延伸字 chamber, stall, room

CV
[ˌsiˋvi]
(n.) 個人簡歷

The interviewer is very pleased with my **CV**.

面試官對我的個人簡歷非常滿意。

延伸字 curriculum vitae, resume

---

deference
[ˈdɛfərəns]
(n.) 服從，遵從

All I ask is your **deference** for the next 2 weeks.

我只要求你們在接下來兩週聽從我的指示。

延伸字 obedience, civility, homage

---

democracy
[dɪˈmɑkrəsɪ]
(n.) 民主政治，
民主國家

Voting is a constitutional right in a country living under **democracy**.

對於民主國家而言，投票是一項憲法保障的權利。

延伸字 equality, freedom, justice

---

designate
[ˈdɛzɪgˌnet]
(v.) 命名，任命

He was **designated** as the next CEO.

他被任命為下一任執行長。

延伸字 name, nominate, appoint

diplomatic

[͵dɪplə`mætɪk]

(adj.) 外交的，
老練的

He is very **diplomatic** when it comes to
negotiating deals.

他在交涉生意上非常的老練。

延伸字 strategic, delicate

---

discrimination

[dɪ͵skrɪmə`neʃən]

(n.) 鑑別，區別，
歧視

Racial **discrimination** will not be tolerated
in this office.

這間辦公室裡不允許任何種族歧視的思
想。

延伸字 discernment, judgment, discretion

---

dismiss

[dɪs`mɪs]

(v.) 解除，免職，
解散

Our plea for shorter working hours has
been **dismissed**.

我們縮短工時的請求被撤回了。

延伸字 sack, terminate, dissolve

---

disparate

[`dɪspərɪt]

(adj.) 不同的，
異類的

The four investigations gave quite
disparate results.

四名調查員提出的調查結果差異非常大。

延伸字 unequal, uneven

MP3
41

○ **disproportionate**

[ˌdɪsprə`porʃənɪt]

(adj.) 不成比例，
　　　不相稱的

The house price is currently **disproportionate** when compared with the average salary.

房價和平均薪資目前相較之下是不成比例的。

延伸字 unreasonable, unequal, inordinate

○ **editor**

[`ɛdɪtɚ]

(n.) 編輯，主筆

He just handed in his piece to the **editor**, and he's pretty nervous.

他剛剛把他的文章交給了編輯，他現在很緊張。

延伸字 editor in chief

○ **eligible**

[`ɛlɪdʒəbl̩]

(adj.) 有資格的，
　　　合適的

It seems like you are **eligible** for the position.

看起來你似乎有資格勝任該職位。

延伸字 qualified, fit, suitable

emphasize

[ˋɛmfəˌsaɪz]

(v.) 加強…的語氣，強調

I cannot **emphasize** more the importance of the regulation on the conduct of business.

我必須極力強調商業行為上管理的重要性。

延伸字 stress, highlight

---

empowerment

[ɪmˋpaʊəˌmənt]

(n.) 活力化

The lightning and the color on the symbol represent **empowerment**.

標誌上的閃電和顏色代表了活力。

延伸字 motivation

---

encourage

[ɪnˋkɝɪdʒ]

(v.) 鼓勵，激勵，支援

My manager always **encourages** me to take on a second language.

我的主管總是鼓勵我去學習第二語言。

延伸字 strengthen, reinforce, revitalize

---

endurance

[ɪnˋdjʊrəns]

(n.) 忍耐力，耐久力

To finish a marathon, you must have very strong **endurance**.

想要跑完馬拉松，你必須具備非常強的耐力。

延伸字 stamina, fortitude

entrepreneur
[ˌɑntrəprəˋnɝ]
(n.) 企業家，
　　創辦人

He regarded himself as an **entrepreneur**.
他認為自己是一位企業家。
延伸字 administrator, founder, executive

excel
[ɪkˋsɛl]
(v.) 優於他人，
　　勝過

One must improve oneself in order to **excel**.
若想要鶴立雞群，必須先提升自己。
延伸字 surpass, exceed, better

exploratory
[ɪkˋsplorəˌtorɪ]
(adj.) 探險的，
　　　探究的

This questionnaire serves an **exploratory** purpose.
這份問卷是為了探索性的目的而製作的。
延伸字 explorative

flatter
[ˋflætɚ]
(v.) 奉承，諂媚

Don't **flatter** yourself; you didn't even do half the work.
少臭美了，你出的力連一半都不到。
延伸字 praise, compliment

fleeting

[ˋflitɪŋ]

(adj.) 短暫的

The photographer successfully captured the **fleeting** moment of the sunrise.

攝影師成功地捕捉到太陽升起的短暫瞬間。

延伸字 transient

---

flexible

[ˋflɛksəbl̩]

(adj.) 有彈性的，靈活的

Remember to keep your mind open and **flexible**.

記得保持一顆開放且靈活的心。

延伸字 manageable, elastic, compromising

---

idolize

[ˋaɪdl̩͵aɪz]

(v.) 將⋯視為偶像

The mayor was **idolized** by many citizens.

許多市民都將市長視為偶像。

延伸字 admire, adore, glorify

---

immigrant

[ˋɪməgrənt]

(n.) 移民，僑民

The country opened its door to **immigrants**.

該國向外來移民開啟了大門。

延伸字 alien, outsider

● **inauguration**

[ɪnˌɔgjəˋreʃən]

(n.) 就職典禮，
就職

He made a beautiful speech during his **inauguration**.

他在就職典禮上發表了一篇非常棒的演說。

延伸字 commencement, initiation

● **inherit**

[ɪnˋhɛrɪt]

(v.) 繼承

I have **inherited** this house from my parents.

我從父母手中繼承了這棟房子。

延伸字 accede, succeed

● **initiative**

[ɪˋnɪʃətɪv]

(n.) 主動性，
主動精神

You need to take **initiative** in order to achieve success.

想要獲得成功，你就必須採取主動。

延伸字 originality, leadership, opening

● **inspirational**

[ˌɪnspəˋreʃən!]

(adj.) 鼓舞的，
啟發的

His actions are very **inspirational** to us.

他的行動對我們來說非常具有啟發性。

延伸字 influential, stimulating

---

instinct

[ˈɪnstɪŋkt]

(n.) 本能，天性

Some people know where a good bargain is to be found by **instinct**.

有些人靠著本能便能找到各種優惠。

延伸字 natural feeling, natural tendency

---

interview

[ˈɪntɚˌvju]

(v.) 接見，訪問，

(n.) 面試

While it's never good to be late for an **interview**, arriving way too early is not great as well.

雖然在面試時遲到很不好，但太早抵達也不是一件好事。

延伸字 examination, communication, consultation

---

labor

[ˈlebɚ]

(v.) 勞動，苦幹

(n.) 勞工

He **labored** 3 months for that project.

他為了那份企劃苦幹了三個月。

延伸字 work, toil, drudge

---

leadership

[ˈlidɚˌʃɪp]

(n.) 領導身分，
　　領導能力

We are all currently under his **leadership**.

我們目前全都跟隨他的領導。

延伸字 headship

magnate

[ˋmægnet]

(n.) 要人，權貴

After our CFO left the company, he became the **magnate** of the stock exchange.

我們的財務長離開公司後，成為了證券交易界的要人。

延伸字 worthy, somebody

---

mentor

[ˋmɛntɚ]

(n.) 良師益友

My high school art teacher has taught me a lot. I consider him my **mentor**.

我的高中美術老師教了我許多事。我一直都把他當作我的恩師。

延伸字 advisor, teacher

---

merit

[ˋmɛrɪt]

(n.) 價值，長處，
優點

Don't just focus on his shortcomings; think about his **merits** as well.

別只是專注在他的缺點，也想想他的長處吧。

延伸字 quality, value, worth

---

motivation

[͵motəˋveʃən]

(n.) 刺激，動機，
行動方式

You just need to find the right **motivation** to complete it.

你只需要找到正確的行動方式來完成它。

延伸字 inspiration, ambition

motto

[ˋmɑto]

(n.) 座右銘，標語

My **motto** is "Never say never".

我的座右銘是「永不說不」。

延伸字 slogan, catchword

---

outstanding

[ˋaʊtˋstændɪŋ]

(adj.) 傑出的，
顯著的

Your work on expanding the product range is **outstanding**.

你在拓展產品範疇方面的工作表現實在是太傑出了。

延伸字 important, great, eminent

---

paparazzi

[ˌpɑpəˋrɑtsɪ]

(n.) 狗仔隊

The celebrity is having an argument with the **paparazzi**.

那名藝人正在和狗仔隊爭執。

延伸字 cameraperson,
　　　 celebrity photographer

---

pension

[ˋpɛnʃən]

(n.) 退休金，年金

He is still waiting for his **pension** to come down.

他仍然在等待領取他的退休金。

延伸字 grant, payment

● **perfectionism**
[pɚˋfɛkʃənɪzm]
(n.) 完美主義，
圓滿論

His **perfectionism** at work can be annoying sometimes.

他工作上的完美主義有時候真的有點煩人。

延伸字 flawlessness, perfectionist

● **potential**
[pəˋtɛnʃəl]
(n.) 潛力
(adj.) 潛在的

It's too bad that he gives up easily. He has so much **potential**.

他那麼輕易就放棄真是太可惜了，他有非常大的潛力。

延伸字 possible, probable

● **privilege**
[ˋprɪvḷɪdʒ]
(n.) 特權，殊榮

Driving is a **privilege**, not a right.

開車是一項特權，而不是一項權利。

延伸字 advantage, benefit, exemption

● **proactive**
[proˋæktɪv]
(adj.) 主動的，
積極的

She is very **proactive** when it comes to her right.

她對於有關自己權益的事總是非常積極。

延伸字 spirited, zealous

promote

[prə`mot]

(v.) 晉升，促進，
發揚

Susan should have been **promoted** three years ago.

Susan 三年前就該獲得晉升了。

延伸字 encourage, inspirit, raise

---

proprietary

[prə`praɪəˌtɛrɪ]

(adj.) 專利的

(n.) 業主，地主

The new product uses a **proprietary** technology.

該新產品使用了一種專利技術。

延伸字 patent, landlord

---

protest

[prə`tɛst]

(v.) (n.) 抗議，反對

We are all gathered here to **protest** against animal cruelty.

我們聚在這是為了抗議虐待動物。

延伸字 objection, challenge, demonstration

---

punctual

[`pʌŋktʃuəl]

(adj.) 守時的，
精確的

He expects his workers to be **punctual**.

他希望員工在工作上守時。

延伸字 punctilious

▶ **punctuality**

[ˌpʌŋktʃʊˈæləti]

(n.) 嚴守時間，
　　正確，規矩

Keep up with your **punctuality**, and there shouldn't be any problems.

繼續嚴守時間，就不會有任何問題。

延伸字 on time, accuracy

▶ **qualification**

[ˌkwɑləfəˈkeʃən]

(n.) 勝任，適合

I'm sorry but you didn't meet our **qualification**.

很抱歉，你並不符合我們的適任條件。

延伸字 competence, fitness, suitability

▶ **qualified**

[ˈkwɑləˌfaɪd]

(adj.) 勝任的，
　　　適當的

Are you sure he is **qualified** to fix this machine?

你確定他有能力去修理這台機器嗎？

延伸字 competent, fit, capable, efficient

▶ **realistic**

[rɪəˈlɪstɪk]

(adj.) 現實的，
　　　實在的

I'm not arguing with you. I just want you to be **realistic**.

我並不是要跟你唱反調。我只是希望你能實際一點。

延伸字 rational, reasonable, practical

---

rebel
[rɪ`bɛl]
(v.) 反抗，反叛

We **rebelled** at having to stay late and check the inventory.
我們對於必須留下來加班檢查庫存表示反對。

延伸字 resist, protest

---

recruitment
[rɪ`krutmənt]
(n.) 徵募新兵，
補充

James went to the **recruitment** center to enlist.
James 為了從軍而前去徵募中心。

延伸字 conscription, draft

---

refugee
[ˌrɛfjʊ`dʒi]
(n.) 流亡者，難民

Refugees are lining up to be sent to a shelter.
難民們排著隊，等候被送往庇護所。

延伸字 outcast, alien, outlaw

---

reimburse
[ˌriɪm`bɝs]
(v.) 付還，償還，
賠償

He gave me two thousand dollars to **reimburse** the damage on my car.
他給我兩千塊來賠償我車子的損壞。

延伸字 refund, offset, return

relapse

[rɪˋlæps]

(v.) 故態萌發，
　復發，惡化

Unfortunately, his illness **relapsed** after 6 months.

很不幸地，他的病在六個月之後又復發了。

延伸字 regress, return, revert

---

relationship

[rɪˋleʃənˋʃɪp]

(n.) 關係，關聯

It's important to maintain a good **relationship** with your customers.

和客戶保持良好的關係是非常重要的。

延伸字 affiliation, association, correlation

---

remainder

[rɪˋmendɚ]

(n.) 剩餘物，
　其餘的人

Don't worry about it. I will take the **remainder** home and finish it.

別擔心，我會把剩下的部分帶回家完成。

延伸字 remnant, remains, the rest

---

remuneration

[rɪˌmjunəˋreʃən]

(n.) 報酬，酬勞

After the piano lesson ended, my mother gave the tutor her **remuneration**.

鋼琴課結束後，我的母親將酬勞交給了老師。

延伸字 salary, earnings, payment

reputation

[ˌrɛpjə`teʃən]

(n.) 名聲

Be mindful of your behavior; we have a **reputation** to keep.

請注意你的行為，我們得顧及我們的名聲。

延伸字 distinction, reliability, character

---

resignation

[ˌrɛzɪg`neʃən]

(n.) 辭職，辭呈

John just handed over his **resignation** this morning.

John 今天早上才剛遞出他的辭呈。

延伸字 termination, withdrawal

---

retire

[rɪ`taɪr]

(v.) 使退休，
　　使退卻

My kids are still in college right now. I don't think it's time for me to **retire**.

我的孩子都還在念大學。現在還不是我能退休的時候。

延伸字 resign, quit, relinquish

---

retirement

[rɪ`taɪrmənt]

(n.) 退休，隱退

After the recent event, I am beginning to think about my **retirement**.

經過最近的事情之後，我開始思考有關退休的事情。

延伸字 retreat, withdrawal, regression

ridiculous

[rɪ`dɪkjələs]

(adj.) 可笑的，
　　　荒謬的

He is so ashamed that he had made a **ridiculous** mistake.

他對於自己過去犯下如此荒謬的錯誤，感到非常羞恥。

延伸字 nonsensical, foolish, preposterous

---

sack

[sæk]

(v.) 解聘，解雇

Unhappy that he was **sacked**, Tom decided to go to court.

Tom 不高興他被解聘了，所以決定上法院。

延伸字 terminate, discharge, dismiss

---

seasoned

[`siznd]

(adj.) 有經驗的，
　　　經過磨練的

The rookie was paired with a **seasoned** worker.

那名新手被安排跟一位經驗豐富的員工搭配。

延伸字 experienced

---

secure

[sɪ`kjʊr]

(v.) 弄到，獲得

We have successfully **secured** the latest smart phone on day one.

我們在第一天便成功地將最新的智慧型手機弄到手。

延伸字 get, obtain, acquire

skeptical

[ˈskɛptɪkl]

(adj.) 懷疑的

Although he trusted the man completely, his wife remained **skeptical**.

雖然他完全信任那位男子，他的太太卻保持懷疑的態度。

延伸字 doubtful

---

skill

[ˈskɪl]

(n.) 能力，本領，
技術

In just a few weeks, he has already demonstrated a great set of **skills**.

在短短幾週內，他已經展現出一連串極佳的能力。

延伸字 ability, talent, gift

---

stationary

[ˈsteʃənˌɛrɪ]

(adj.) 不動的，
定居的

The stock price has remained almost **stationary** for the past 2 days.

股價在過去兩天之間幾乎毫無變化。

延伸字 fixed, immovable, immobile

---

struggle

[ˈstrʌgl]

(v.) 努力，掙扎，
奮鬥

We've been **struggling** ever since the economic crisis.

自從金融危機之後，我們就一直在掙扎著。

延伸字 conflict, encounter

○ **subordinate**

[səˋbɔrdṇɪt]

(adj.) 下級的

(n.) 部屬

A **subordinate** should respect those who are above him.

下屬應該要對上級表現出尊重的態度。

延伸字 dependent, secondary

○ **subsidize**

[ˋsʌbsəˏdaɪz]

(v.) 給予津貼，
補助

The company paid me some money to **subsidize** my trip.

公司付我一些錢來補助我的行程。

延伸字 sponsor, fund, contribute

○ **success**

[səkˋsɛs]

(n.) 成功，成就，
勝利

In order to achieve **success**, one must be sure of himself.

想要獲得成就，就必須相信自己。

延伸字 attainment, achievement

○ **supremacy**

[səˋprɛməsɪ]

(n.) 最優地位，
最高權威

The navy has demonstrated their **supremacy** on the sea.

海軍在海上展現出他們的絕對優勢。

延伸字 superiority

surgery

[ˋsɝdʒərɪ]

(n.) 手術

Frank is currently still in **surgery**, and we are really worried.

Frank 目前仍然在手術中，我們真的很擔心。

延伸字 operation

---

tier

[tɪr]

(n.) 層，列，段

Workers from different **tiers** are responsible for different issues.

來自不同層級的員工將負責處理不同的問題。

延伸字 story, layer, level

---

trendy

[ˋtrɛndɪ]

(adj.) 時髦的

Cindy always looks so **trendy**. She really does have fashion sense.

Cindy 隨時隨地看起來都好時髦。她真的很有時尚品味。

延伸字 stylish, fashionable, latest, popular

---

unemployment

[ˌʌnɪmˋplɔɪmənt]

(n.) 失業人數，失業

The **unemployment** rate of this city is slowly rising.

這座城市的失業率正緩緩攀升中。

延伸字 joblessness

○ **union**
[ˋjunjən]
(n.) 同盟，工會，
聯合

The **union** is trying to negotiate better pay for the workers.

工會正在為提升員工薪資而試著進行談判。

延伸字 combination, congregation, consolidation

○ **unscrupulous**
[ʌnˋskrupjələs]
(adj.) 無道德的，
狂妄的

He lied to us all! What an **unscrupulous** man!

他居然騙了我們所有人！真是一個沒道德的傢伙！

延伸字 dishonest, unprincipled

○ **upfront**
[ˋʌpˏfrʌnt]
(adj.) 直率的，
坦白的

I really wish my husband could be more **upfront** with me.

我很希望我先生可以對我再坦白一點。

延伸字 frank, honest

○ **vibrant**
[ˋvaɪbrənt]
(adj.) 鮮明的，
活耀的

Her painting is always so **vibrant** and heart-warming.

她的畫作總是那麼的鮮明又溫暖。

延伸字 lively

wage

[wedʒ]

(n.) 薪水，報酬

I have been earning the minimum **wage** for the past 3 years.

過去三年間我都只領最低薪資。

延伸字 pay, payment, salary

---

weakness

[`wiknɪs]

(n.) 弱點，虛弱，脆弱

We need to find their **weakness** before we strike.

我們必須先找出對方的弱點才能出擊。

延伸字 feebleness, frailty, inability

---

workaholic

[ˌwɝkə`hɔlɪk]

(n.) 醉心工作者，工作狂

My husband is a **workaholic**, and he always brings his work back home.

我先生是一個工作狂，他總是把工作帶回家。

延伸字 workhorse, peon

8

專案進行
Special Projects

How many words do you know?
你知道這些字的意思和用法嗎？

- [ ] arbitration
- [ ] impasse
- [ ] obstacle
- [ ] severance
- [ ] stalemate
- [ ] tactfully

abandon

[əˋbændən]

(v.) 遺棄，中止，放棄

After much discussion, we decided to **abandon** this project.

討論許久之後，我們決定中止這項企劃。

延伸字 leave, forsake, discontinue

---

accomplishment

[əˋkɑmplɪʃmənt]

(n.) 完成，結束，實現

It's best to give children a sense of **accomplishment** during class.

在課堂上最好能讓孩子們獲得成就感。

延伸字 fulfillment, realization, success

---

activate

[ˋæktəˏvet]

(v.) 啟動，活化

I tried to **activate** the garage door, but it wouldn't move.

我試著啟動車庫的門，但它一動也不動。

延伸字 prompt, start, trigger

---

adjourn

[əˋdʒɝn]

(v.) 中止，延期

The case was **adjourned** until next week.

那項案件被延到下週。

延伸字 end, suspend, recess

adjustment

[ə`dʒʌstmənt]

(n.) 調整，調節，校正

Her **adjustment** to the new environment is very fast.

她在新環境裡調適的速度非常快。

延伸字 modification, improvement, alteration

---

analysis

[ə`næləsɪs]

(n.) 分析，分解，解析

The unknown substance was sent to the lab for **analysis**.

該不明物質被送到實驗室做解析。

延伸字 examination, discussion

---

arbitration

[ˌɑrbə`treʃən]

(n.) 仲裁，調定，公斷

The union finally agreed to go to **arbitration** as a way of ending the strike.

工會終於同意以進行仲裁的方式來結束罷工。

延伸字 conclusion, determination

---

argument

[`ɑrgjəmənt]

(n.) 爭執，論點，爭吵

I don't like it when I get into an **argument** with someone.

我不喜歡自己和別人起爭執的狀況發生。

延伸字 disagreement, questioning, controversy

atmosphere

[ˋætməsˌfɪr]

(n.) 大氣，氣氛，
氛圍

The **atmosphere** of that church is very warm and welcoming.

那間教堂的氣氛令人感到非常溫暖且友善。

延伸字 surroundings, ambiance, feeling

---

audit

[ˋɔdɪt]

(v.) 審核，查帳

The company is sending people over to **audit** the factory.

公司將派遣人員來查核工廠。

延伸字 examine, review, check

---

backward

[ˋbækwɚd]

(adj.) 落後的

Those are some very **backward** thoughts.

那都是些非常落後的想法。

延伸字 behindhand

---

brainstorming

[ˋbrenˌstɔrmɪŋ]

(n.) 集體研討

We spent the whole afternoon **brainstorming**.

我們花了一整個下午進行集體研討。

延伸字 discussion, consultation

chaotic

[keˋɑtɪk]

(adj.) 混亂的，
亂七八糟的

The traffic will be pretty **chaotic** during the holidays.

假日的交通將會變得非常混亂。

延伸字 confused, disordered, disorganized

---

circulate

[ˋsɝkjəˌlet]

(v.) 傳播，傳遞，
發行

Money shall **circulate** freely within the common market.

資金會在共同市場內自由流通。

延伸字 publish, broadcast

---

comprise

[kəmˋpraɪz]

(v.) 由…組成，
包括

Our team **comprises** a project leader, two consultants, and three specialists.

我們團隊由一位專案經理，兩位顧問和三位專員組成。

延伸字 include, contain, involve

---

compromise

[ˋkɑmprəˌmaɪz]

(v.) 妥協，讓步，
放棄

We value our customers, so we will not **compromise** our quality.

我們很重視我們的客戶，因此我們不會在品質上妥協。

延伸字 settle, yield

○ **concede**
[kən`sid]
(v.) 承認，容許

She was forced to **concede** that he might be right.
她被迫勉強承認他可能是對的。

延伸字 admit, allow, grant

○ **concession**
[kən`sɛʃən]
(n.) 讓步，承認，
特許

You need **concession** from the government to chop the wood here.
你需要政府許可才能砍伐這裡的樹木。

延伸字 allowance, admission, compromise

○ **concise**
[kən`saɪs]
(adj.) 簡潔的，
簡明的

When briefing the board members, remember to be **concise**.
向董事會成員做簡報時，記得內容要簡單明瞭。

延伸字 compact, brief, succinct

○ **conclude**
[kən`klud]
(v.) 結束

This **concludes** our event for tonight. Please join us tomorrow.
今晚的活動已結束，請於明天再加入我們。

延伸字 close, end, finish, stop

concrete

[`kankrit]

(adj.) 具體的

We still need **concrete** evidence to prove what really happened.

我們仍需要具體的證據來證明實際上發生了什麼事。

延伸字 substantive, tangible

---

conglomerate

[kən`glamərit]

(n.) 聚集物，
企業集團

The larger companies are mostly part of multinational **conglomerates**.

規模較大的公司通常都是跨國企業的一部分。

延伸字 compound

---

constitute

[`kanstə,tjut]

(v.) 組成，任命，
構成

Our company is **constituted** by 6 departments.

我們的公司是由六個部門所組成的。

延伸字 complement, incorporate, integrate

---

deadlock

[`dɛd,lak]

(n.) 僵局

(v.) 停頓

Our negotiation was stuck in a **deadlock**.

我們的談判陷入僵局。

延伸字 cessation, dead end, standstill

○ debate

[dɪˋbet]

(n.) (v.) 辯論，討論

We had a heated **debate** on the company's future.

我們針對公司的未來進行了一場激烈的辯論。

延伸字 discuss, argue, dispute

○ debut

[dɪˋbju]

(n.) 初次登台，
　　首次亮相

The singer just released her **debut** album last month.

那名歌手上個月才剛剛發行她的第一張專輯。

延伸字 admission, entrance

○ determination

[dɪˏtɝməˋneʃən]

(n.) 決定，判定

I am not responsible for the **determination** of your salary.

我並不負責決定你的薪水。

延伸字 decision, adjudication

○ devote

[dɪˋvot]

(v.) 奉獻於，
　　專心於

He **devoted** his whole life to marine research.

他將一輩子的時間奉獻在海洋研究上。

延伸字 dedicate, consecrate

digression

[daɪˋɡrɛʃən]

(n.) 離題，脫軌

Such **digressions** can lead us too far afield.

這樣離題下去會讓我們越扯越遠。

延伸字 abnormality, departure

---

dilute

[daɪˋlut]

(v.) 稀釋，使薄弱

If the alcohol is too strong, you can use soda water to **dilute** it.

如果酒太烈，你可以加點蘇打水來稀釋它。

延伸字 weaken, reduce, thin

---

disband

[dɪsˋbænd]

(v.) 解散

The idol group **disbanded** last year due to in-group disputes.

那個偶像團體在去年因為內部紛爭而解散了。

延伸字 separate, scatter, disperse

---

discard

[dɪsˋkɑrd]

(v.) 放棄

We are forced to **discard** our whole project because of him.

因為他，我們被迫放棄整項企劃。

延伸字 desert, abandon

● **effective**

[ɪˋfɛktɪv]

(adj.) 有效的，
有力的

A friendly and warm attitude is an **effective** way to gain a customer's trust.

既友善又熱情的態度，能有效贏得客戶的信任。

延伸字 practical, compelling, operative

● **efficient**

[ɪˋfɪʃənt]

(adj.) 效率高的，
有效的

When tackling a project, it's best to find the most **efficient** way to work on it.

處理企劃案時，最好找出一種最有效率的工作方式。

延伸字 effective, active, operative

● **evidence**

[ˋɛvədəns]

(n.) 證據，證詞，
跡象

We found **evidence** that he stole from the company.

我們找到他竊取公司資源的證據。

延伸字 fact, proof, sign

● **extract**

[ɪkˋstrækt]

(v.) 精萃，摘錄，
擷取

They've been **extracting** minerals from that mine.

他們從那個礦坑中挖掘礦物。

延伸字 concentrate, withdraw, distill

focus

[ˋfokəs]

(n.) 焦點

(v.) 專注

We should try not to lose the **focus** of this discussion.

我們應該盡量不要偏離這場討論的焦點。

延伸字 concentration, spotlight, core

---

illuminating

[ɪˋlumənetɪŋ]

(adj.) 照明的

The **illuminating** lamp post is the only light source here.

照明的路燈是這裡唯一的光源。

延伸字 clarifying

---

impasse

[ˋɪmpæs]

(n.) 死路，僵局

The negotiations had reached an **impasse**.

該場交涉已陷入了僵局。

延伸字 deadlock, standstill, stalemate

---

improvement

[ɪmˋpruvmənt]

(n.) 改進，改善

There is always room for more **improvement**.

總是還有更多改善的空間。

延伸字 advancement, enhancement, progression

○ inconsiderately

[͵ɪnkən`sɪdərətlɪ]

(adv.) 不經考慮地

He **inconsiderately** parked the car on the side of the road.

他毫不考慮他人便將車子停在路旁。

延伸字 recklessly

○ interaction

[͵ɪntə`rækʃən]

(n.) 互相影響，
互動

Don't be a workaholic; go out and enjoy some human **interaction**.

別當工作狂了，去外頭享受一點與人們的互動吧。

延伸字 interactive

○ intervention

[͵ɪntə`vɛnʃən]

(n.) 插手，介入，
調停

We are really looking forward to the government's **intervention**.

我們很期望政府能夠插手介入。

延伸字 intercession, interference

○ irreconcilable

[ɪ`rɛkən͵saɪləbl̩]

(adj.) 不能和解的
，對立的

Their differences seem **irreconcilable**.

他們似乎無法化解彼此的差異。

延伸字 incompatible

judge

[dʒʌdʒ]

(v.) 審判，判決，
評斷

Don't be too quick to **judge** a person solely by his looks.

別單看外表就很快地評斷一個人。

延伸字 referee, decide, consider

---

maintenance

[ˋmentənəns]

(n.) 維護，保持，
維修

It's been a while since our servers had any **maintenance**.

我們的伺服器已經一陣子沒有維護了。

延伸字 conservation, preservation, upkeep

---

mission

[ˋmɪʃən]

(n.) 使命，任務

When the person in charge gives you a **mission**, it is your job to complete it.

當負責人將任務交給你，你的使命就是完成任務。

延伸字 errand, business, task

---

mortgage

[ˋmɔrgɪdʒ]

(n.) 抵押，貸款

I still have to pay this **mortgage** for another 20 years.

我仍然得繼續支付貸款 20 年。

延伸字 contract, debt, pledge

multiple
[ˋmʌltəpḷ]
(adj.) 複合的，
多樣的

Karen is amazing. She could take on **multiple** things at once.
Karen 真是厲害。她可以一次處理好多件事。

延伸字 compound, manifold

---

narrow
[ˋnæro]
(adj.) 狹窄的，
被限制的

I am trying to squeeze through the **narrow** walkway.
我正試著擠過那條狹窄的走道。

延伸字 slender, close, tight

---

nomination
[ˌnɑməˋneʃən]
(n.) 提名，任命

The **nomination** of the upcoming president is still not out yet.
下一任總統的提名人選還沒有公佈。

延伸字 designation, recommendation

---

obstacle
[ˋɑbstəkḷ]
(n.) 障礙，阻礙

I think most of these **obstacles** can be overcome.
我認為這些阻礙大部分都可以被克服。

延伸字 barrier, obstruction

occasion

[əˈkeʒən]

(n.) 時機，機會，
場合

You dressed up nicely. What's the special **occasion**?

你打扮得真漂亮。是要參加什麼特殊的場合嗎？

延伸字 affair, function, opportunity

---

ongoing

[ˈɑnˌɡoɪŋ]

(adj.) 仍在進行的

The investigation is still **ongoing**. We'll contact you if something comes up.

調查仍然在進行中。如果有任何進展我們會通知你的。

延伸字 continual, progressive

---

opposition

[ˌɑpəˈzɪʃən]

(n.) 反抗，對立，
對手

We have successfully defeated the **opposition**.

我們成功地擊敗了對手。

延伸字 competition, resistance,
　　　　 confrontation

---

opt

[ɑpt]

(v.) 選擇

If you like, you can always **opt** out of the program.

如果你想要，隨時都可以選擇退出這項計畫。

延伸字 choose, select

outcome
[ˋaʊtˌkʌm]
(n.) 結果，結局

I'm sorry, but the **outcome** isn't very ideal.
很抱歉，結果並不是很理想。
延伸字 result, consequence, conclusion

---

overload
[ˌovɚˋlod]
(v.) 使負荷過多，
使超載

Hurry up and turn it off; you're **overloading** the machine.
快點將它關掉，你讓機器負荷太重了。
延伸字 overstress

---

portfolio
[portˋfolɪˌo]
(n.) 文件夾，
公事包

Someone left his or her **portfolio** on the bus.
有人將他的公事包留在公車上了。
延伸字 briefcase

---

postpone
[postˋpon]
(v.) 使延期，延緩

All people are too busy. It won't hurt to **postpone** the meeting.
大家現在都很忙，把會議延後應該沒有太大影響。
延伸字 delay, defer, suspend

preliminary

[prɪˈlɪməˌnɛrɪ]

(adj.) 預備的，
　　　開始的

Don't worry. We just need to run some **preliminary** tests.

別擔心，我們只是需要做點預先測試。

延伸字 preparatory, prefatory, opening

---

process

[ˈprɑsɛs]

(n.) 過程，進程，
　　　程序

Successfully getting a business deal can be a lengthy **process**.

要成功地獲得一筆生意，其過程可能會相當漫長。

延伸字 operation, procedure, step

---

project

[ˈprɑdʒɛkt]

(n.) 方案，規劃，
　　　工程

After a short break, we are ready to take on our next **project**.

短暫休息過後，我們已經準備好接手下一個案子。

延伸字 assignment, design, scheme

---

rearrange

[ˌriəˈrendʒ]

(v.) 重新整理，
　　　再排列

I think we need to **rearrange** the decorations of our booth.

我認為我們需要重新裝飾我們的攤位。

延伸字 reorder, shift, revamp

○ **reasonable**

[ˋriznəbl]

(adj.) 通情達理的
，合理的

If you could give us a **reasonable** price, we will make the order right here right now.

如果你可以給我們一個合理的價格，我們現在馬上就能下訂。

延伸字 sensible, logical, rational

▶ **referee**

[͵rɛfəˋri]

(n.) 裁判，仲裁

The **referee** blew the whistle and issued a red card.

裁判吹了哨子並發出一張紅牌。

延伸字 judge, moderator, umpire

▶ **regularly**

[ˋrɛgjələˋlɪ]

(adv.) 有規律地，
定期地

He **regularly** oils and maintains his bicycle.

他定期地為他的腳踏車上油及保養。

延伸字 periodically, usually

▶ **repel**

[rɪˋpɛl]

(v.) 擊退，排斥

My mom bought an insect repellent to **repel** cockroaches.

我媽買了一罐殺蟲劑來對付蟑螂。

延伸字 repulse, offend, revolt

retain
[rɪˋten]
(v.) 保留，維持

Even after all these years, she still **retains** her beauty.
就算在這麼多年之後，她仍然維持著她的美麗。

延伸字 keep, hold, maintain

---

rigid
[ˋrɪdʒɪd]
(adj.) 堅硬的，
　　　堅固的

The wall is so **rigid** that we couldn't even scratch its surface.
那面牆堅硬到連稍微刮傷它都沒辦法。

延伸字 stiff, firm, hard, unbending

---

settle
[ˋsɛtl̩]
(v.) 解決，和解，
　　　安頓

There's no need to get rough. You can always **settle** this through a more civilized fashion.
沒有必要動粗。你可以用更文明的方式來解決這件事。

延伸字 determine, decide, resolve

---

settlement
[ˋsɛtl̩mənt]
(n.) 協議

According to our **settlement**, you have to pay for my car's damage.
根據我們的協議，你必須支付我車輛損壞的費用。

延伸字 agreement, arrangement

○ **severance**

[ˋsɛvərəns]

(n.) 切斷，隔離，
契約解除

Henna received a **severance** package after she was laid off.

Henna 被資遣後收到了一筆資遣費。

延伸字 cutting

○ **solid**

[ˋsɑlɪd]

(adj.) 實心的，
堅固的

Although this table is already 50 years old, it is still very **solid**.

雖然這張桌子已經有 50 年了，它仍然非常堅固。

延伸字 concentrated, substantial

○ **stage**

[stedʒ]

(n.) 時期，階段

We all have different responsibilities during the different **stages** of our lives.

我們人生的不同階段，都有不一樣的責任需要完成。

延伸字 period, interval, time, point

○ **stalemate**

[ˋstelˌmet]

(n.) 僵局，困境，
膠著

We need to try and break the **stalemate**.

我們必須試著打破僵局。

延伸字 delay, pause, impasse

stimulation

[ˌstɪmjəˋleʃən]

(n.) 刺激

Whenever I want some **stimulation** in the morning, I drink a coffee.

每當我早上想來點提神的東西時，我就喝一杯咖啡。

延伸字 incentive, stimulant

---

subject

[ˋsʌbdʒɪkt]

(n.) 主題，科學，科目

When in a meeting, please remember to keep the **subject** of the conversation on topic.

開會時，請記得將談話的主題著重在議題上。

延伸字 topic, theme, issue

---

symbolize

[ˋsɪmbḷˌaɪz]

(v.) 代表，象徵

The logo **symbolizes** hope and strength.

那個標誌象徵了希望與力量。

延伸字 signify, stand for

---

systematically

[ˌsɪstəˋmætɪkḷɪ]

(adv.) 有組織地，有系統地

The manager wants us to think about this project **systematically**.

經理要我們有系統地去思考這項企劃。

延伸字 methodically

● **tactfully**

[ˋtæktfəlɪ]

(adv.) 機智地，
巧妙地

Jerry dealt with an awkward situation very **tactfully**.

Jerry 很巧妙地化解了一個尷尬的場面。

延伸字 masterfully, smartly

● **term**

[tɝm]

(n.) 術語，詞條，
條件

If you have any doubt, please read our **terms** and conditions first.

若您有任何疑慮，請先參閱我們的條款及條件。

延伸字 arrangement, condition

● **transaction**

[trænˋzækʃən]

(n.) 辦理，交易

The **transaction** is final, no refunds.

這項交易已經完成，恕不退款。

延伸字 deal, sale

● **turmoil**

[ˋtɝmɔɪl]

(n.) 騷動，混亂

The country is in **turmoil** right now.

這個國家目前正處於動亂之中。

延伸字 confusion, violence, disturbance

verify

[ˈvɛrəˌfaɪ]

(v.) 證明，證實

Before making any decisions, remember to **verify** all the facts first.

在做出任何決定之前，記得先驗證所有資料的真實性。

延伸字 confirm, prove, validate

---

worksheet

[ˈwɝkˌʃit]

(n.) 工作表單，
備忘錄

The boss was not satisfied with the **worksheet** we just delivered, and asked us to modify it.

老闆對我們剛剛交出去的工作表不是很滿意，要求我們做修改。

---

workshop

[ˈwɝkˌʃɑp]

(n.) 專題討論會，
研討會

We are discussing the possibility of starting a writing **workshop**.

我們正在談論成立寫作研習會的可能性。

延伸字 seminar

9

客戶服務
Customer Service

How many words do you know?
你知道這些字的意思和用法嗎？

- [ ] collision
- [ ] escalate
- [ ] neutral
- [ ] patron
- [ ] reconcile
- [ ] unsolicited

● **accumulate**

[əˋkjumjəˌlet]

(v.) 累積，收集

She has **accumulated** a lot of wealth over the past few years.

她在過去幾年間累積了不少財富。

延伸字 gather, amass, compile

● **accustom**

[əˋkʌstəm]

(v.) 使習慣於

After working beside her for 8 years, I am pretty much **accustomed** to her daily habits.

在她身旁工作八年之後，我差不多已經適應她的日常習慣了。

延伸字 addict, condition, familiarize

● **affordable**

[əˋfɔrdəbl]

(adj.) 買得起的，
負擔得起的

The man is trying to find an **affordable** car.

那位男子正在找一輛他負擔得起的車子。

延伸字 sustainable

● **alternative**

[ɔlˋtɝnətɪv]

(n.) 選擇，替代

They had no **alternative** but to close the store.

他們別無他法，只能將店關起來。

延伸字 choice, substitute, replacement

anonymous

[əˋnɑnəməs]

(adj.) 不具名的，
匿名的

We just received an **anonymous** tip
regarding this case.

我們剛剛收到一個跟這個案件有關的匿名
消息。

延伸字 incognito, secret

---

anxious

[ˋæŋkʃəs]

(adj.) 焦慮的，
掛念的

He is **anxious** about the speech later
because he is not well prepared.

因為他沒有準備好，所以對待會兒的演說
感到非常焦慮。

延伸字 uneasy, concerned, fearful

---

appliance

[əˋplaɪəns]

(n.) 裝置，器具，
設備

My wife is asking for a set of new kitchen
appliances.

我太太要求我買一組新的廚房設備。

延伸字 tool, instrument

---

bizarre

[bɪˋzɑr]

(adj.) 古怪的，
奇特的

The patterns on this ancient vase are
bizarre.

這個古老花瓶上的花樣還真奇怪。

延伸字 peculiar, odd

○ **casual**

[ˋkæʒʊəl]

(adj.) 非正式的，
不拘禮的

Calling people by customers' first names is considered too **casual** or overly familiar.

直呼客戶的名字，可能會顯得太隨便或被認為是在裝熟。

延伸字 informal, random, unexpected

○ **client**

[ˋklaɪənt]

(n.) 顧客，客戶

Adam is currently out meeting with a **client**.

Adam 目前外出與一位客戶會面。

延伸字 customer, prospect, patron

○ **collision**

[kəˋlɪʒən]

(n.) 衝突，抵觸

The **collision** between the two planes is due to a radar malfunction.

兩架飛機相撞的原因是因為雷達故障。

延伸字 argument, battle, conflict

○ **commitment**

[kəˋmɪtmənt]

(n.) 承諾，委託，
奉獻，投入

His **commitment** to helping the needy is very touching.

他致力於幫助需要幫助的人，非常令人感動。

延伸字 liability, promise, engagement

competitor

[kəm`pɛtətɚ]

(n.) 競爭對手

Recently, many customers are leaving **competitors** to use our service.

最近有很多客戶都捨棄競爭對手，並改用我們的產品了。

延伸字 rival

---

complain

[kəm`plen]

(v.) 抱怨，埋怨，不滿

He always **complains** about his job, and never tries to improve himself.

他總是在抱怨自己的工作，卻從未試著改善自己的能力。

延伸字 criticize, contravene, disagree

---

conform

[kən`fɔrm]

(v.) 遵照，符合

Employees should **conform** to the company's policy.

員工應該要遵守公司的政策。

延伸字 comply, agree, assent

---

controversial

[ˌkɑntrə`vɝʃəl]

(adj.) 具爭議性的

His opinions have always been extremely **controversial**.

他所表達的意見向來都非常具有爭議性。

延伸字 argumentative, questionable

core
[kor]
(n.) 核心，精髓

Distractions from the **core** mission may take away the company's focus.
跟公司的主要任務無關的事會模糊焦點。

延伸字 kernel, center, essence

---

critic
[`krɪtɪk]
(n.) 評論家，
　　批評家

The food **critic** is pretty satisfied with the dishes there.
美食評論家對於那些菜餚感到相當滿意。

延伸字 arbiter, connoisseur, judge

---

criticism
[`krɪtə͵sɪzəm]
(n.) 批評，評論

Not all **criticism** is negative.
並非所有的批判都是負面的。

延伸字 evaluation, judgment, assessment

---

customize
[`kʌstəm͵aɪz]
(v.) 自訂，訂製，
　　客製化

The bakery let me **customize** my own cake.
麵包店讓我客製化自己的蛋糕。

延伸字 tailor-made

defect

[dɪˋfɛkt]

(n.) 缺點，缺陷

He was born with a birth **defect**, but it never took him down.

他出生時便帶有天生的缺陷，但他從來都沒有被它打敗。

延伸字 fault, flaw, weakness

---

device

[dɪˋvaɪs]

(n.) 設備，儀器，裝置

We've just brought in a lot of expensive **devices** into the lab.

我們才剛為實驗室引進許多昂貴的儀器。

延伸字 machine, apparatus, tool

---

digest

[daɪˋdʒɛst]

(v.) 消化，領悟

Before responding to my client, I always take a few seconds to **digest** the information.

在回覆客戶之前，我總是會花一些時間消化資訊。

延伸字 absorb, comprehend, catch on

---

disappoint

[ˌdɪsəˋpɔɪnt]

(v.) 使失望

I am very sorry to **disappoint** you all.

我很抱歉讓你們大家失望了。

延伸字 dissatisfy, displease, let down

○ **dispute**
[dɪ`spjut]
(v.) 爭論，爭執

People are **disputing** over the cause of this problem.

人們正在為這項問題的起因爭論著。

延伸字 argue, debate, quarrel

○ **distinct**
[dɪ`stɪŋkt]
(adj.) 有區別的，
　　　不同的

Companies, like individuals, have a **distinct** personality.

公司如同個人，都有自己獨特的特質。

延伸字 different, dissimilar, diverse

○ **distraction**
[dɪ`strækʃən]
(n.) 注意力分散，
　　　分心

I'm not really happy right now. I need some **distraction**.

我現在不是很開心。我需要一些能讓我分心的事。

延伸字 diversion, abstraction

○ **eliminate**
[ɪ`lɪməˌnet]
(v.) 除去，排除，
　　　消除

We seek to **eliminate** our competition by using this product.

我們希望藉由這個產品來排除競爭對手。

延伸字 terminate, discard, discharge

escalate

[ˈɛskəˌlet]

(v.) 上升，升級

I need to **escalate** this issue to higher levels.

我需要將此事件呈報上級。

延伸字 broaden, enlarge, extend

---

essential

[ɪˈsɛnʃəl]

(adj.) 不可或缺的，必要的

Providing great services to customers is an **essential** part of our company's corporate culture.

「為客戶提供優良服務」是我們公司企業文化中不可或缺的一部分。

延伸字 necessary, vital, required

---

exaggerate

[ɪgˈzædʒəˌret]

(v.) 誇大

Don't believe her; she's just **exaggerating** the truth.

別相信她，她只是在誇大事實而已。

延伸字 overstate

---

expectation

[ˌɛkspɛkˈteʃən]

(n.) 期望，期待

Customers' **expectations** for good service run awfully high.

客戶對優良服務的期望是相當高的。

延伸字 anticipation, prospect

greeting

[ˋgritɪŋ]

(n.) 問候，迎接，
招呼

We can always receive a quick, friendly **greeting** in that retail store.

在那間零售店，我們總是能得到迅速又友善的接待和問候。

延伸字 welcome, salutation, regards

---

guarantee

[͵gærənˋti]

(v.) 保證

Buying a bus ticket doesn't **guarantee** you a seat.

買到公車票並不保證你就有座位可坐。

延伸字 promise, pledge, assure

---

hassle

[ˋhæsḷ]

(n.) 麻煩，困難

We will get our problem solved with no **hassle** and no delay.

我們會簡單地解決問題，絕不拖延。

延伸字 difficulty, inconvenience

height

[haɪt]

(n.) 高度

The benefits of good customer service will carry our company to greater **heights** and healthier profits.

優良客服的好處是可以讓我們的事業更創高峰，帶來更多利潤。

延伸字 pinnacle

---

ignore

[ɪgˋnor]

(v.) 忽略

He is always rude like that; just **ignore** him.

他向來都是那麼無禮，別理他就好。

延伸字 neglect, overlook

---

immediate

[ɪˋmidɪət]

(adj.) 立即的，
　　　馬上的

We expect to get an **immediate** answer that actually solves our problem.

我們期望立即得到可以真正解決問題的答案。

延伸字 straightaway, right away

---

implement

[ˋɪmpləmənt]

(v.) 實施，執行

If you **implement** the strategies and ideas we offered, you will profitably stand out.

若您採納我們提供的策略和意見，您的業務會做得很出色。

延伸字 carry out, bring about

innovation
[ˌɪnə`veʃən]
(n.) 革新，創新

Our management prefers to see money invested in product and service **innovations**.

我們的管理階層期望資金可以投資在產品和服務的創新上。

延伸字 leading edge, modernism

---

install
[ɪn`stɔl]
(v.) 安置，安裝

The technicians are here to **install** new computers for us.

技術人員是來幫我們安裝新電腦的。

延伸字 establish, admit

---

irritate
[`ɪrə͵tet]
(v.) 使惱怒，
使煩躁

My neighbor's lifestyle really **irritates** me.

我鄰居的生活方式使我感到很煩躁。

延伸字 annoy, incite, agitate

---

keen
[kin]
(adj.) 熱切的，
熱心的

When top management shows a **keen** interest in the operation, everyone else tends to pay attention, too.

當高階管理者展現出對公司營運的熱切關心，員工才會跟進。

延伸字 eager

lasting

[ˈlæstɪŋ]

(adj.) 永久性的

We aim to have a **lasting** presence in the market.

我們的目標是在市場上永久存續。

延伸字 persistent

---

loyalty

[ˈlɔɪəltɪ]

(n.) 忠誠，忠貞，忠實

Our team leader has inspired **loyalty** in many.

我們的團隊領導者有許多忠實的支持者。

延伸字 integrity, reliability, attachment

---

measurable

[ˈmɛʒərəbl̩]

(adj.) 可測量的，重大的

When you create a culture of service, the results present themselves in **measurable** ways.

當你創造出一種服務文化，可量化的成果便會顯示出來。

延伸字 perceptible, weighable, assessable

---

method

[ˈmɛθəd]

(n.) 方法，辦法

In order to communicate effectively, we need to use different **methods** in communicating with different people.

要能有效地溝通，我們就必須對不同的人採取不同的溝通方式。

延伸字 system, means, scheme

modify
[ˋmɑdəˌfaɪ]
(v.) 修改，修正，
變更

He **modified** my report and used it as his own.

他修改了我的報告，並且挪為己用。

延伸字 change, alter, transform

---

neutral
[ˋnjutrəl]
(adj.) 中立的

Our manager likes to get members to talk informally in a **neutral**, stress-free environment.

我們經理希望所有團隊成員都可以在一個中立、無壓力的環境中暢所欲言。

延伸字 impartial, indifferent, independent

---

particular
[pɚˋtɪkjələ˞]
(adj.) 特殊的，
特定的

I'll divide my presentation into several major parts, and each will focus on a **particular** aspect of delivering good service.

我將我的演講分成幾個主要的部分，每部分則針對提供優良服務的內容，鎖定一個特定面向提出見解。

延伸字 specific, distinct

patron

[ˋpetrən]

(n.) 顧客，主顧

We have a special offer for our regular **patrons**.

我們有一項只提供給主顧客的特別優惠。

延伸字 customer, client, frequenter

---

percentage

[pɚˋsɛntɪdʒ]

(n.) 百分比

A small **percentage** of your customer base may account for the vast majority of your profits.

一小部分的客戶群，可能是公司大部分利潤的來源。

延伸字 proportion, ratio, rate

---

persuasion

[pɚˋsweʒən]

(n.) 說服，勸服，誘惑

The client could be so stubborn sometimes. No **persuasion** can get through those ears.

那位客戶有時候真的很固執，任何勸說都聽不進去。

延伸字 inducement, suasion, advice

---

petition

[pəˋtɪʃən]

(n.) 請求，申訴

A lot of us went ahead and signed the **petition**.

我們很多人都去簽署了那份請願書。

延伸字 request, demand, appeal

please
[pliz]
(v.) 使高興，討好

We've spent a lot of time **pleasing** demanding customers.

我們花了很多時間取悅苛求的客戶。

延伸字 gratify, satisfy

---

pledge
[plɛdʒ]
(n.) 誓言，諾言

The mayor made a **pledge** to erase street violence.

市長承諾要解決在街上發生的各種暴力事件。

延伸字 promise, vow, oath

---

prejudice
[ˋprɛdʒədɪs]
(n.) 偏見，成見

Don't let your **prejudice** affect your judgment.

別讓你的偏見影響到你的判斷。

延伸字 animosity, antipathy

---

pressure
[ˋprɛʃɚ]
(n.) 壓力，緊迫

Many people under time **pressure** believe they don't have enough time to handle a problem well.

很多在時間壓力下工作的人，認為自己沒有充足的時間可以妥善解決問題。

延伸字 force, burden, influence

primary

[`praɪ‚mɛrɪ]

(adj.) 首要的，
主要的

Our **primary** goal for this quarter is to increase our revenue by 10%.

我們本季的首要目標是要將營收提升百分之十。

延伸字 first, important, chief, main

---

promise

[`prɑmɪs]

(v.) 承諾

(n.) 諾言

The mayor **promises** to reduce the crime rate by half this time next year.

市長承諾在明年此時犯罪率將會減半。

延伸字 agree, pledge, vow

---

realize

[`rɪə‚laɪz]

(v.) 瞭解，領悟

Successful businesses **realize** they cannot be all things to all people.

成功的企業瞭解，他們不可能滿足所有人的全部需求。

延伸字 understand, grasp, comprehend

---

reconcile

[`rɛkən‚saɪl]

(v.) 和解，改善

After a few days of fighting, they've decided to **reconcile**.

吵了幾天的架之後，他們決定和解了。

延伸字 settle, harmonize

redeem
[rɪ`dim]
(v.) 履行，挽救

You can still **redeem** yourself by confessing to the police.
你仍然可以藉由向警方自首來挽救自己。

延伸字 fulfill, rescue, recover

---

reduction
[rɪ`dʌkʃən]
(n.) 減少，縮減

The **reduction** of our budget this year is pretty bad.
我們今年的預算縮減狀況真的很糟。

延伸字 decrease, loss, cutback

---

reference
[`rɛfərəns]
(n.) 提及，涉及，
　　參考，推薦函

My previous employer gave me a really good **reference**.
我之前的雇主給了我一份非常好的推薦信。

延伸字 mention, notice, suggestion

---

refund
[rɪ`fʌnd]
(v.) 償還，退款

The shopkeeper **refunded** all the money to the angry customer.
店家將所有錢退回給那位憤怒的客人。

延伸字 repay, reimburse, pay back

reliable
[rɪˋlaɪəbl]
(adj.) 可靠的

Our mission is to design highly **reliable** products.

我們的使命是要設計可靠度高的產品。

延伸字 trustworthy, dependable, safe

---

repetitive
[rɪˋpɛtɪtɪv]
(adj.) 重複的

This job requires a great deal of **repetitive** work with little variation.

這份工作重覆性很高，不太有變化性。

延伸字 constant, dull, monotonous

---

require
[rɪˋkwaɪr]
(v.) 需要，需求

Improvement is an ongoing process that **requires** thorough analysis.

不斷進步是持續進行的，還需要徹底的分析。

延伸字 necessitate, demand, need

---

resistance
[rɪˋzɪstəns]
(n.) 耐力，反抗，抵抗力

His **resistance** to the cold is amazing.

他對寒冷的抵抗力真是驚人。

延伸字 obstruction, contention, safeguard

◗ **respect**

[rɪˋspɛkt]

(v.) (n.) 尊重

Our management tries to make all employees feel valued and **respected**.

我們的管理階層試著讓所有員工感到有價值和受尊重。

延伸字 adore, appreciate, honor

◗ **rewarding**

[rɪˋwɔrdɪŋ]

(adj.) 有益的，
　　　有回報的

Customer service can be a challenging profession, but also an extremely **rewarding** one.

客戶服務是很有挑戰性的一種專業，但同時也有極大的回饋。

延伸字 satisfying, fruitful

◗ **sanity**

[ˋsænətɪ]

(n.) 清醒，明智

If I feel down for whatever reason, I will take a **sanity** break and get some fresh air.

不論什麼原因讓我心情不佳，我都會休息充電一下並呼吸新鮮空氣。

延伸字 acumen, clear mind, stability

scanner

[`skænɚ]

(n.) 掃描機

Since we don't have a digital copy of the file, I have to use a **scanner** and make one.

由於我們沒有該檔案的電子版本，我必須用掃描機製作一份。

---

scrap

[skræp]

(n.) 片段，碎片，殘餘物

For my childhood, I can only recall **scraps** of memories.

對於我的童年，我只能回想起一些片段的回憶。

延伸字 fragment, portion, remains

---

serious

[`sırıəs]

(adj.) 嚴重的，嚴肅的

From the look of his face, we realized the situation is very **serious**.

我們從他的表情就能得知，情況非常嚴重。

延伸字 important, weighty, grave

---

serve

[sɝv]

(v.) 為⋯服務

We consider it a privilege and a joy to **serve** you.

可以為您服務是我們莫大的榮幸。

延伸字 help, assist

specific

[sprˋsɪfɪk]

(adj.) 明確的，
特有的

(n.) 詳情

Enough with the small talk. It's time to get into the **specifics**.

別再閒聊了，我們開始談細節吧。

延伸字 definite, precise, special

---

subscribe

[səbˋskraɪb]

(v.) 訂閱，訂購，
認捐

Remember to encourage the customer to **subscribe** to our newsletter.

記得鼓勵那位客戶訂閱我們的電子報。

The company **subscribes** to local charities every month.

公司每個月都會捐款給當地的慈善機構。

延伸字 support, contribute

---

technician

[tɛkˋnɪʃən]

(n.) 技術人員，
技師

The repair **technician** showed up at our business to fix our copier just 20 minutes after we called for service.

在我們打電話要求維修的二十分鐘後，技術人員就抵達我們辦公室修理影印機了。

延伸字 specialist, expert, pro

tedious

[ˋtidɪəs]

(adj.) 乏味的，
使人厭煩的

That meeting was **tedious**; I almost fell asleep.

那場會議實在很枯燥乏味，我差點就睡著了。

延伸字 dull, dreary, slow, dry

---

tend

[tɛnd]

(v.) 傾向，易於

We **tend** to react to others based on our own behavioral style.

我們總是傾向依照自己的行事風格來跟人互動。

延伸字 incline, lean

---

toxic

[ˋtɑksɪk]

(adj.) 毒性的，
有毒的

The water is **toxic**; I wouldn't drink it if I were you.

水有毒，如果我是你的話就不會喝。

延伸字 poisonous, deadly, venomous

---

treat

[trit]

(v.) 對待

Everyone who comes in contact with our company wants to be **treated** nicely and promptly.

每位前來洽公的客戶，都希望得到友善的對待和迅速的回應。

延伸字 handle

treatment
[`tritmənt]
(n.) 處理，治療，
對待

My husband is responding really well to the **treatment**.
我先生對於治療的反應非常良好。
延伸字 management, process, care

unique
[ju`nik]
(adj.) 獨特的

Every organization has its own **unique** culture.
每個企業都擁有自己獨特的文化。
延伸字 distinctive

unsolicited
[ˌʌnsə`lɪsɪtɪd]
(adj.) 未經同意的

The transaction in question is **unsolicited**.
這項討論中的交易尚未經過許可。
延伸字 undesirable, unsought, not requested

upgrade
[ˌʌp`gred]
(v.) 升級，提升，
改良

To ask for better pay, one must try and **upgrade** oneself first.
若想要求更好的待遇，就必須先努力提升自己的能力才行。
延伸字 increase, advance, enhance

vaccinate

[ˋvæksn͵et]

(v.) 打疫苗，
預防接種

He took his dog to the vet to have it **vaccinated**.

他將狗帶去獸醫院打疫苗。

延伸字 inject, mitigate, prevent

---

vested

[ˋvɛstɪd]

(adj.) 賦予的，
既定的

Freedom is **vested** in all of us.

自由屬於我們每一個人。

延伸字 bestow

---

vitally

[ˋvaɪtəlɪ]

(adv.) 極為，十分

All team members need to understand what good service is and why it's so **vitally** important.

所有的成員都應該瞭解什麼是好的服務，以及好的服務為何如此重要。

延伸字 significantly, imperatively

---

vocal

[ˋvokl̩]

(adj.) 口頭表示，
直言不諱的

The demanding customer is no doubt the most **vocal** customer.

要求多的客戶毫無疑問就是會直言不諱的客戶。

延伸字 voiced, spoken, articulate

○ **vulnerable**

［`vʌlnərəbl̩］

(adj.) 易受傷的，
　　　脆弱的

He just endured a breakup, and is pretty **vulnerable** right now.

他才剛剛經歷分手，現在內心還很脆弱。

延伸字 defenseless, weak

○ **worthwhile**

［`wɝθ`hwaɪl］

(adj.) 值得的，
　　　有價值的

I'm sure in the end these will all be **worthwhile**.

我相信到最後，這些全都會是值得的。

延伸字 beneficial, profitable, meritorious

10 Business Operations

How many words do you know?
你知道這些字的意思和用法嗎？

- [ ] allegation
- [ ] contemporary
- [ ] embezzlement
- [ ] forgery
- [ ] insolvent
- [ ] redundant

acquisition
[ˌækwəˈzɪʃən]
(n.) 獲得，取得

He spent three months on the **acquisition** of this information.
他花了三個月才取得這項資訊。

延伸字 purchasing, takeover, obtainment

---

adjacent
[əˈdʒesənt]
(adj.) 鄰近的，
鄰接的

Our company is **adjacent** to the main train station. It's in the center of the city.
我們公司鄰近主要的火車站，位於這個都市的中心地帶。

延伸字 neighboring, adjoining

---

aftermath
[ˈæftɚˌmæθ]
(n.) 後果，餘波

The **aftermath** of the earthquake is heartbreaking.
地震後的現場令人感到心碎。

延伸字 consequence, fallout

---

allegation
[ˌæləˈgeʃən]
(n.) 指控，斷言，
主張

He disputed all the illegal **allegations** against him.
他駁回了所有針對他的非法指控。

延伸字 affirmation, declaration, accusation

ambassador
[æmˋbæsədɚ]
(n.) 大使，使節

The **ambassador** was asked to brief the president.
該位大使被要求向總統作簡報。

延伸字 diplomat, emissary

---

assessment
[əˋsɛsmənt]
(n.) 評價，估計，
估價

Our initial **assessment** on this product is pretty poor.
我們針對這個產品的初步評價並不是很好。

延伸字 judgment, estimate, charge

---

attainment
[əˋtenmənt]
(n.) 達到，獲得，
到達

The **attainment** of wealth did not make her happy.
成功獲得了財富並沒有使她感到快樂。

延伸字 success, accomplishment, completion

---

automated
[ˋɔtometɪd]
(adj.) 自動化的，
機械化的

Our operator has been replaced by an **automated** switchboard.
我們的接線員已被自動化的總機所取代。

延伸字 automatic

bankruptcy
[`bæŋkrəptsɪ]
(n.) 破產，倒閉

After 10 years, the company finally declared **bankruptcy**.

經過 10 年之後，該公司終於宣布破產。

延伸字 failure

---

boardroom
[`bord,rum]
(n.) 董事會會議室

I feel nervous every time I step into the **boardroom**.

我每次踏進董事會會議室時都會感到緊張。

---

bureaucracy
[bjʊ`rakrəsɪ]
(n.) 官僚政治

People are getting very sick of the **bureaucracy** now.

人們對於官僚政治已經感到非常厭煩了。

延伸字 government

---

capital
[`kæpətl]
(n.) 資金，首府
(adj.) 主要的

We are moving to the **capital** city of our country.

我們要搬到我們國家的首都去了。

延伸字 investment, fundamental

chain

[tʃen]

(n.) 鍊條，一連串

(v.) 拘禁

The bankruptcy of the company led to a **chain** of events.

公司的破產導致一連串事件的發生。

延伸字 bind, restrain, fasten

---

collapse

[kə`læps]

(v.) 倒塌，崩潰

The old building **collapsed** right in front of my eyes.

那棟老建築就在我眼前垮下來了。

延伸字 fail, crash, topple

---

combine

[kəm`baɪn]

(v.) 使結合，
　　使聯合

My knowledge **combined** with your technique and we will make a great team.

將我的知識與你的技術結合，我們將會成為非常棒的團隊。

延伸字 join, unite, mix, associate

---

commit

[kə`mɪt]

(v.) 犯（罪），
　　做（錯事）

When an employee **commits** fraud, the company must take immediate action.

當員工犯下欺詐的行為時，公司必須立即做出處置。

延伸字 perform, do

community
[kə`mjunətɪ]
(n.) 社會，族群，共同體

My friend was sentenced to **community** service for cursing at others.
我的朋友因為對別人罵髒話，而被判社區服務。

延伸字 association, territory, affinity

---

competition
[‚kampə`tɪʃən]
(n.) 競爭

A little **competition** between brands is always good for consumers.
品牌之間的一些競爭對消費者而言是好的。

延伸字 opposition, rivalry

---

confusion
[kən`fjuʒən]
(n.) 混亂，騷動

In order to avoid **confusion**, we each tied a red band on our sleeves.
為了避免混亂，我們每個人都在袖子上綁了一條紅布。

延伸字 bewilderment, perplexity

---

constraint
[kən`strent]
(n.) 約束，限制，抑制

It takes a lot of self-**constraint** to lose weight.
減重需要強大的自我約束力。

延伸字 detention, repression, control

contemporary

[kən`tɛmpə͵rɛrɪ]

(adj.) 同時代的，
現代的

I always have a hard time understanding **contemporary** art.

我總是沒辦法了解現代藝術。

延伸字 concurrent, up-to-date

---

contingency

[kən`tɪndʒənsɪ]

(n.) 可能性，
意外事故

You need to have a **contingency** plan in case something happens.

為了預防萬一，你必須要有應付突發事故的計劃。

延伸字 probability, likelihood

---

copyright

[`kɑpɪ͵raɪt]

(n.) 版權，著作權

Our company owns the **copyrights** of several logos you are using.

本公司擁有你正在使用的數個標誌的版權。

延伸字 patent, license

---

corruption

[kə`rʌpʃən]

(n.) 腐敗，墮落，
貪污

The organization is filled with **corruption** and greed.

組織內充滿了腐敗與貪婪。

延伸字 degradation, depravity, distortion

○ **counteract**

[ˌkaʊntɚˋækt]

(v.) 對抗，抵消，
起反作用

We initiated an emergency plan to **counteract** their new service.

我們發起了一項緊急計劃來對抗他們的新服務。

延伸字 contradict, oppose, act against

○ **crisis**

[ˋkraɪsɪs]

(n.) 緊要關頭，
危機

We are currently under the biggest **crisis** this company has ever seen.

我們目前正處於公司有史以來最大的危機。

延伸字 catastrophe, emergency,
confrontation

○ **declaration**

[ˌdɛkləˋreʃən]

(n.) 宣佈，宣告，
聲明

The company's **declaration** of bankruptcy struck us by surprise.

公司的破產聲明讓我們全都吃了一驚。

延伸字 announcement, publication,
communication

○ **default**

[dɪˋfɔlt]

(n.) (v.) 不履行，
棄權，
拖欠

She **defaulted** from the tournament due to personal reasons.

基於個人因素，她從錦標賽中棄權了。

延伸字 delinquency

deployment
[dɪ`plɔɪmənt]
(n.) 部署，配置

We need to reconsider our **deployment** of stores.
我們需要重新評估店面的配置。

延伸字 formation, implementation, organization

---

depreciate
[dɪ`priʃɪˌet]
(v.) 貶值，降價

Your mistake is that you let the value of your house **depreciate** too much.
你的錯誤就是你讓這間房子的價錢貶值太多了。

延伸字 underestimate, belittle

---

devastating
[`dɛvəsˌtetɪŋ]
(adj.) 破壞性極大的

The impact of the scandal is **devastating**.
醜聞的打擊具有非常大的破壞性。

延伸字 disastrous, destructive

---

diagnose
[`daɪəgnoz]
(v.) 診斷，分析

His illness was **diagnosed** as cancer.
他的病情被診斷為癌症。

延伸字 interpret, analyze, deduce

dominate
[ˈdɑməˌnet]
(v.) 支配，統治，控制

Our cat has **dominated** our living room.
我們家的客廳已經被我們的貓所佔據了。

延伸字 control, rule, command

---

downplay
[ˈdaʊnple]
(v.) 不予重視，貶低

Please don't **downplay** your effort during this campaign.
請不要貶低你自己為這場活動所付出的努力。

延伸字 lessen, play down, soften

---

embezzlement
[ɪmˈbɛzḷmənt]
(n.) 盜用公款，挪用

He was sentenced to jail for **embezzlement**.
他因盜用公款的罪名被判決入獄服刑。

延伸字 financial fraud

---

establishment
[əˈstæblɪʃmənt]
(n.) 建立，設立，創立

My father helped me a lot during the **establishment** of my company.
在公司成立的期間，我父親幫助我很多。

延伸字 foundation, constitution

evolution

[ɛvəˈluʃən]

(n.) 進展，發展，
進化

We are all fascinated by the **evolution** of their products.

我們全都對他們產品的發展史感到著迷。

延伸字 progression, change, growth

---

executive

[ɪgˈzɛkjʊtɪv]

(adj.) 經營的，
管理的

I am trying to get promoted to an **executive** position.

我正試著讓自己晉升到管理職位。

延伸字 directing, managing, administrative

---

failure

[ˈfeljɚ]

(n.) 失敗，疏忽，
失敗者

This deal is extremely important; **failure** is not an option.

這筆生意非常重要，絕對不能失敗。

延伸字 crash, collapse, fiasco

---

fierce

[fɪrs]

(adj.) 凶猛的，
殘酷的

That's a **fierce** dog you have there. Please don't let him run free.

你的狗還真凶猛。請不要讓牠四處亂跑。

延伸字 ferocious, violent, raging

fiercely

[ˋfɪrslɪ]

(adv.) 猛烈地，
厲害地

The two companies have been competing **fiercely** over the new market.

這兩間公司為了新的市場，競爭相當激烈。

延伸字 frantically, severely, hard

---

fiscal

[ˋfɪskl̩]

(adj.) 財政的，
會計的

The first month of a **fiscal** year is not necessarily the same as a regular year.

財政年度的第一個月和一般年度的月份不一定相同。

延伸字 financial, commercial

---

forgery

[ˋfɔrdʒərɪ]

(n.) 偽造，贗品

Remember to check the money first; they might be **forgeries**.

記得先檢查一下這些錢，它們可能是偽造的。

延伸字 copy, duplication, replication

---

fragment

[ˋfrægmənt]

(n.) 碎片，破片

We are only able to recover **fragments** of the statue.

我們只能找回雕像的碎片。

延伸字 part, portion, segment

framework

[ˈfremˌwɝk]

(n.) 結構，組織，架構

We need to reestablish our decision-making **framework**.

我們必須重新建構我們的策略制定架構。

延伸字 structure, scheme, frame

---

franchise

[ˈfrænˌtʃaɪz]

(v.) 給予特權

(n.) 經銷權

A **franchised** restaurant just opened across the street.

一間連鎖餐廳最近在對街開幕了。

延伸字 privilege, charter, freedom

---

fulfillment

[fʊlˈfɪlmənt]

(n.) 完成，履行，實現

We are still waiting for the **fulfillment** of his promise.

我們仍然在等待他實現諾言。

延伸字 success, performance, content

---

governance

[ˈgʌvɚnəns]

(n.) 統治，管理，統治權

Corporate **governance** is not something that anyone could master.

企業管理並不是一件任何人都可以勝任的事情。

延伸字 administration, execution, authority

gravity

[ˈɡrævətɪ]

(n.) 重大，嚴肅，危險性

Please don't joke about this. You have no idea the **gravity** of the situation.

請不要拿這件事開玩笑。你根本不知道狀況的嚴重性。

延伸字 severity, importance

---

guideline

[ˈɡaɪdˌlaɪn]

(n.) 指導方向，指標

It is only a **guideline**. Remember to make your own judgment.

那只是個原則。記得要自己做判斷。

延伸字 instruction, guidance, rule of thumb

---

hamper

[ˈhæmpɚ]

(v.) 妨礙，阻擾，約束

Our progress was **hampered** by the bad weather.

我們的進度因為天候狀況不佳而受阻。

延伸字 hinder, impede, cramp, obstruct

---

heritage

[ˈhɛrətɪdʒ]

(n.) 繼承，遺傳

I have some European **heritage** and that's why I've got blue eyes.

我有歐洲血統，這就是我有藍眼睛的原因。

延伸字 heredity, birthright

impact

[ɪm`pækt]

(n.) 衝擊，影響，作用

The economic crisis in the U.S. had a great **impact** on our company.

美國的經濟危機對我們公司產生了非常大的衝擊。

延伸字 collision, clash

---

implementation

[ˌɪmpləmɛn`teʃən]

(n.) 實行，履行，啟用

It will take a while before the **implementation** of a new system could set in.

全新啟用的系統需要一段磨合的時間。

延伸字 application, utilization, fulfillment

---

incur

[ɪn`kɝ]

(v.) 招致，蒙受，遭遇

On my first day, I **incurred** my boss's displeasure.

我第一天上班就惹得老闆不高興。

延伸字 provoke, obtain, arouse

---

inevitably

[ɪn`ɛvətəblɪ]

(adv.) 不可避免，必然地

Inevitably, our children have to leave home one day.

不可避免地，我們的孩子總有一天必須離開這個家。

延伸字 surely

infrastructure

[ˋɪnfrəˌstrʌktʃɚ]

(n.) 基礎構造，
基本建設

The workers are the **infrastructure** of this company.

員工才是這間公司的基礎。

延伸字 framework, base, root

insolvent

[ɪnˋsɑlvənt]

(adj.) 無力償還的
，破產的

The company is basically **insolvent**. I'm sure of it.

我很肯定這間公司基本上已經破產了。

延伸字 broken, indebted, unbalanced

legal

[ˋligl̩]

(adj.) 法律上的，
合法正當的

I assure you that this whole process is **legal**.

我向你保證整個流程都是合法的。

延伸字 lawful, legitimate, valid

license

[ˋlaɪsn̩s]

(n.) 許可，特許，
執照

You need a liquor **license** to sell alcohol.

你需要酒類營業執照才能販售酒類商品。

延伸字 permission, allowance, consent

manage

[ˈmænɪdʒ]

(v.) 管理，經營，處理

Don't worry about me. I'll **manage** it somehow.

別擔心我，我會設法處理的。

延伸字 control, conduct, handle

---

meltdown

[ˈmɛltˌdaʊn]

(n.) 崩潰，瓦解

After so many days of overtime, she's really close to a **meltdown**.

在連續加班了好幾天之後，她已經快要崩潰了。

延伸字 downfall, devastation

---

merger

[ˈmɝdʒɚ]

(n.) 合併，歸併

I've heard the people up top are chatting about some sort of **merger**.

我聽說上頭的人正在討論有關公司合併的事情。

延伸字 combination, alliance, organization

---

methodology

[ˌmɛθəˈdɑlədʒɪ]

(n.) 方法論，教學法

I can spend the whole day explaining the **methodology** of systems engineering to you.

我可以花上一整天的時間解釋系統工程學方法論給你聽。

misconduct

[mɪsˋkandʌkt]

(n.) 不規矩，
不良行為

The student was sent home for **misconduct**.

該名學生因為行為不良而被開除了。

延伸字 delinquency, error, criminality

---

operate

[ˋapəˏret]

(v.) 運轉，營運，
操作

Currently, Hank is the only one that knows how to **operate** this thing.

目前 Hank 是唯一知道如何操作這東西的人。

延伸字 work, run, perform, function

---

operation

[ˏapəˋreʃən]

(n.) 操作，經營，
作用

The **operation** of this store is crucial to our success.

這間店面的營運，對我們的成功是非常重要的。

延伸字 employment, utilization, execution

outlook

[ˋaʊtˌlʊk]

(n.) 前景，展望，見解

After a successful product launch, I say the **outlook** for our company is pretty good.

在產品成功推出之後，我認為我們公司的前景非常好。

延伸字 prospect, expectation, opportunity

---

parliament

[ˋpɑrləmənt]

(n.) 議會，國會

The **parliament** is having a heated debate right now.

國會目前正在進行激烈的辯論。

延伸字 legislature, congress, senate

---

politician

[ˌpɑləˋtɪʃən]

(n.) 政治家，政客

Never trust a **politician**, for they only care about their fame and fortune.

永遠不要相信政客，因為他們只在乎自己的聲望與財產。

延伸字 diplomat

---

preclude

[prɪˋklud]

(v.) 妨礙，阻止

The traffic jam **precluded** me from attending the meeting.

塞車造成我無法參加會議。

延伸字 forbid, prohibit

proclamation

[͵prɑklə`meʃən]

(n.) 宣佈，公告，宣言

The **proclamation** of the merger surprised everyone.

有關合併的宣布讓大家都吃了一驚。

延伸字 declaration, broadcast, notice

---

production

[prə`dʌkʃən]

(n.) 產量，產品，生產

I am happy to announce the product is finally in **production**.

我很高興宣佈該產品已經開始生產。

延伸字 generation, output, yield

---

property

[`prɑpətɪ]

(n.) 財產，資產，房產

Please try to not damage the company's **property**.

請試著避免破壞公司資產。

延伸字 possession, holdings, belongings

---

publication

[͵pʌblɪ`keʃən]

(n.) 發表，公佈，出版物

The interview with our CEO was printed in several **publications** today.

我們執行長的訪談於今天登上了數本出版品的版面。

延伸字 announcement, communication, declaration

redundant

[rɪˋdʌndənt]

(adj.) 多餘的，
過剩的

The company is laying off all the **redundant** workers.

公司正在資遣所有的冗員。

延伸字 needless, excessive

---

reform

[͵rɪˋfɔrm]

(v.) 改革

After the layoffs, it's time to **reform** the company's structure.

資遣之後，就是開始對公司架構進行改革的時候了。

延伸字 change

---

regulate

[ˋrɛgjə͵let]

(v.) 管理，控制，
調整

Remember to **regulate** your breathing while jogging.

在慢跑時記得調整自己的呼吸。

延伸字 manage, govern, handle, direct

---

regulation

[͵rɛgjəˋleʃən]

(n.) 規章，規則，
規定

There are plenty of **regulations** on employees' working hours.

有許多針對員工工時所制定的規定。

延伸字 rule, order, command, directive

● **relinquish**
[rɪ`lɪŋkwɪʃ]
(v.) 放棄，撤出

He **relinquished** the chance to be promoted.
他放棄了晉升的機會。

延伸字 give up, surrender

● **renew**
[rɪ`nju]
(v.) 重新開始，
更新

My client wishes to **renew** his contract with us.
我的客戶希望跟我們更新他的合約。

延伸字 resume, recommence

● **reorganize**
[ri`ɔrgə͵naɪz]
(v.) 改組，改造，
再編制

Our company tried to **reorganize** itself, and laid off several workers.
我們公司試著重新更改編制，並裁掉了數名員工。

延伸字 revamp, regroup

● **revolutionize**
[͵rɛvə`luʃən͵aɪz]
(v.) 徹底改造

Our product has **revolutionized** the industry.
我們的產品徹底改造了這個產業。

延伸字 change, reform

○ **scandal**

[`skændl̩]

(n.) 醜聞，中傷，流言

The **scandal** made him step off his position.

醜聞使他離開了原本的職位。

延伸字 disgrace, wrongdoing, discredit

○ **shareholder**

[`ʃɛrˌholdɚ]

(n.) 股東

Our **shareholders** are very concerned about the recent stock price drop.

我們的股東非常在意近日股價的下跌。

延伸字 shareowner

○ **standoff**

[`stændˌɔf]

(adj.) 冷淡的

(n.) 和局，僵持

After a tense **standoff**, the criminals have decided to surrender.

在一場緊張的對峙之後，罪犯決定投降。

延伸字 tie, draw, reserved

○ **substantiate**

[səb`stænʃɪˌet]

(v.) 證實

The theory was **substantiated** by scientific evidence.

該學說已獲得科學證據證實。

延伸字 confirm, prove

- **sway**

  [swe]

  (v.) 搖擺，動搖

  She is trying very hard to **sway** him from his decision.

  她很努力地試著讓他改變主意。

  延伸字 swing, influence, affect

- **transparency**

  [træns`pɛrənsɪ]

  (n.) 透明度，透明

  Transparency in decision-making is very important for a democratic country.

  對於民主國家而言，決策制定的透明化是非常重要的。

  延伸字 clarity

- **untenable**

  [ʌn`tɛnəb!]

  (adj.) 無法防守，
        站不住腳的

  We have been forced to an **untenable** position.

  我們被逼到了一個無法防守的位置。

  延伸字 indefensible

單字實力測驗
Vocabulary Test

Knowledge is a treasure, but practice is the key to it.

知識是一座寶庫，實踐是打開寶庫的鑰匙。

Test 1

Q1. My name is Lily Chen. I have an _____ with Ms. Anderson at 3.
- (A) affirmation
- (B) appointment
- (C) excellence
- (D) application

Q2. It's a(n) _____ to meet you, Mr. Steve.
- (A) strategy
- (B) opportunity
- (C) fortune
- (D) pleasure

Q3. Our company has its _____ in Singapore.
- (A) rooms
- (B) wrinkles
- (C) beverage
- (D) headquarters

Q4. Our _____ product manager will speak at this conference, as the manager is on business travel.
- (A) deputy
- (B) depressed
- (C) domestic
- (D) disnatured

Q5. Our manager's spacious new office _____ the city.

    (A) overwhelmed

    (B) overlooked

    (C) overcame

    (D) overruled

Q6. Anna Chen's mystery novels have a _____ audience in Taiwan.

    (A) developed

    (B) tremendous

    (C) demanding

    (D) physical

Q7. I have a _____ of miniature dolls.

    (A) collection

    (B) contribution

    (C) resolution

    (D) promotion

Q8. The meeting will be _____ to our new product launch.

    (A) interesting

    (B) deserted

    (C) delighted

    (D) conducive

Q9. The boardroom is _____ by sales department.

(A) impressed

(B) occupied

(C) closed

(D) rejected

Q10. After watching the sunset, I was left with a very _____ feeling.

(A) severe

(B) peaceful

(C) sleepy

(D) serious

Q11. In Taipei, people have to move quickly to _____ the cars in the streets.

(A) process

(B) dodge

(C) control

(D) cause

Q12. In many companies, the person who fails to collaborate well with team members is likely to be _____ by others.

(A) isolated

(B) preserved

(C) encouraged

(D) promoted

Q13. I am forever _____ for your kind assistance.

    (A) dependent

    (B) grateful

    (C) optimistic

    (D) constant

Q14. My position on this issue is _____.

    (A) casual

    (B) unusual

    (C) punctual

    (D) unchangeable

Q15. During the rainy season, we sometimes have a whole month of _____ rain.

    (A) defective

    (B) continuous

    (C) prolific

    (D) violent

Q16. George is one of my _____ relatives.

    (A) native

    (B) realistic

    (C) bloody

    (D) distant

Q17. Lack of sleep is _____ to your health.

    (A) harmful

    (B) annoying

    (C) puzzling

    (D) faithful

Q18. Self-confidence is a(n) _____ factor for success.

    (A) familiar

    (B) negative

    (C) essential

    (D) minor

Q19. It is a mistake to _____ that riches always bring happiness.

    (A) suppose

    (B) show

    (C) appear

    (D) introduce

Q20. It is a fact that Mr. Hill is quite _____. It's not easy to change his mind.

    (A) breakable

    (B) inaccurate

    (C) tolerant

    (D) inflexible

Q1. I intend to discuss our XPM project and _____ a preliminary proposal for your attention.

(A) charge

(B) handle

(C) enclose

(D) modify

Q2. If you require any further information, please do not _____ to contact me.

(A) hesitate

(B) receive

(C) include

(D) believe

Q3. Thanks for your email asking for ways of increasing sales morale. Please find _____ document with specific plans for this.

(A) attaches

(B) attached

(C) attachment

(D) attaching

Q4. Following our phone conversation last week, I am writing to
_____ that I can speak at next month's conference.

(A) reform

(B) transform

(C) elicit

(D) confirm

Q5. Our company has a _____ format for writing letters to clients.

(A) standing

(B) standard

(C) standardize

(D) stands

Q6. I am looking forward to your _____ response.

(A) prompt

(B) promotion

(C) promote

(D) promptly

Q7. We _____ the problem you experienced with the Z493
model.

(A) guide

(B) please

(C) occupy

(D) regret

Q8. I am writing to _____ our next PPM meeting to review our projects.

(A) organized

(B) organize

(C) organization

(D) organizing

Q9. Please confirm your arrival details so that I can _____ for someone to pick you up at the airport.

(A) finish

(B) arrange

(C) conduct

(D) submit

Q10. Please let me know as soon as possible if these dates are _____.

(A) convenient

(B) professional

(C) standard

(D) pleasant

Q11. This letter is to confirm your _____ at the quarterly training workshop to be held in Taipei.

(A) autonomy

(B) endorsement

(C) enrollment

(D) notice

Q12. Payments made after October 3rd will result in _____ fees being added to the registration fee.

(A) overlook

(B) overdue

(C) overwhelm

(D) overrule

Q13. Using plain language and less _____ will make the report clearer.

(A) jargon

(B) credibility

(C) vocabulary

(D) plan

Q14. I _____ recommend that you check the email once again.
before you send it out.

(A) fortunately

(B) professionally

(C) sharply

(D) strongly

Q15. With the advent of the Internet, many companies are now
_____ products online.

(A) marketing

(B) making

(C) progressing

(D) delivering

Q16. Mr. Smith asked me to _____ to his message as soon as
possible.

(A) rewrite

(B) return

(C) retrieve

(D) reply

Q17. Did you have a _____ to look over my report, Sherry?

(A) proof

(B) chance

(C) period

(D) energy

Q18. The _____ sales report must be finished by the end of next month.

(A) annual

(B) frequent

(C) practical

(D) useful

Q19. We did not get the _____, because we missed the deadline.

(A) communication

(B) confirmation

(C) contract

(D) construction

Q20. It took four workers three days to _____ the task.

(A) complete

(B) accommodate

(C) approve

(D) compare

Q1. Can you put me through to _____ 333, please?

(A) extension

(B) expansion

(C) expiration

(D) exterior

Q2. We must have a bad connection because I keep hearing an

_____ on the line.

(A) attention

(B) echo

(C) objective

(D) urgency

Q3. Is there anything else we need to discuss _____ our project?

(A) rearrange

(B) reorganize

(C) retrieve

(D) regarding

Q4. Could you please give Mr. Thomson a _____ for me when he

gets in?

(A) mirage

(B) message

(C) massage

(D) marriage

Q5. My assistance called the airline to _____ my tickets.

(A) verification

(B) verify

(C) verified

(D) verifying

Q6. I'm afraid you've reached the wrong department. I'll _____ you back to the operator.

(A) call

(B) service

(C) transfer

(D) change

Q7. You can reach marketing department by _____ "7" now.

(A) writing

(B) submitting

(C) talking

(D) dialing

Q8. Due to a _____ problem, the office phones won't be working for the next 20 minutes.

(A) technical

(B) noisy

(C) thorough

(D) wonderful

Q9. After you arrive, just ask for Ms. Wilson at the _____ desk.

(A) employee

(B) reception

(C) office

(D) assistance

Q10. Please tell him it is _____ that he calls me back before noon.

(A) essential

(B) aggressive

(C) polite

(D) complex

Q11. Your report only has a few _____ statements.

(A) ambiguous

(B) impossible

(C) necessary

(D) reimburse

Q12. My boss handed me an _____ before my day off.

(A) assignment

(B) admission

(C) extension

(D) indication

Q13. The time of the interview is not _____ for me.

    (A) fortunate

    (B) polite

    (C) appropriate

    (D) useful

Q14. Mary is a very _____ person to work with.

    (A) forgetful

    (B) agreeable

    (C) elderly

    (D) generous

Q15. Mr. Jones' factory _____ us with raw materials.

    (A) disturbs

    (B) supplies

    (C) responds

    (D) reflects

Q16. Are you familiar with the _____ for purchasing stationery?

    (A) procedure

    (B) donation

    (C) harmony

    (D) ambiance

Q17. Tom follows orders well, but he seldom _____ action.

    (A) urges

    (B) expresses

    (C) initiates

    (D) implies

Q18. This factory _____ 3,000 laptops a month.

    (A) produces

    (B) pushes

    (C) plans

    (D) bakes

Q19. I will send you a _____ of the document.

    (A) purchase

    (B) category

    (C) duplicate

    (D) permission

Q20. This _____ analysis supported my main points.

    (A) conservative

    (B) critical

    (C) realistic

    (D) overdue

Q1. After working for two hours, Alice spent the _____ of the afternoon relaxing.

(A) pastime

(B) minority

(C) remainder

(D) balance

Q2. He _____ a car accident due to his quick reflexes.

(A) produced

(B) happened

(C) caused

(D) prevented

Q3. The _____ of the gigantic hotel began last year.

(A) intersection

(B) construction

(C) circulation

(D) duration

Q4. As a result of the expansion of the public transportation system, our company will _____ our shuttle bus service.

(A) celebrate

(B) emerge

(C) discontinue

(D) complete

Q5. The _____ left the town in complete disorder.

    (A) hurricane

    (B) guidance

    (C) insurance

    (D) content

Q6. The company aims at making _____ products.

    (A) disperse

    (B) bustling

    (C) dramatic

    (D) innovative

Q7. Henry has been working _____ for decades.

    (A) overseas

    (B) concisely

    (C) outright

    (D) hereby

Q8. The lake _____ in the middle of the park is calm today.

    (A) satisfied

    (B) situated

    (C) evaluated

    (D) bounded

Q9. The caterers must know _____ how many people are expected.

(A) approximately

(B) confidentially

(C) similarly

(D) separately

Q10. The building was _____ within a very short time.

(A) evacuated

(B) authorized

(C) displayed

(D) liberated

Q11. People who live in that developed country enjoy a(n) _____ lifestyle.

(A) complicated

(B) impractical

(C) deluxe

(D) difficult

Q12. It took me five hours to reach the _____ in such a rainy day.

(A) destination

(B) appreciation

(C) reservation

(D) conclusion

Q13. Miss Lu _____ that her car was hit by a van.

    (A) entices

    (B) softens

    (C) claims

    (D) cancels

Q14. We had a lovely visit because the Jones was so _____.

    (A) rude

    (B) hospitable

    (C) tolerable

    (D) confusing

Q15. Shy people are often _____ at parties and other social gatherings.

    (A) overlooked

    (B) overrated

    (C) overseen

    (D) overtaken

Q16. Last night I went to a concert given by a group of _____ musicians.

    (A) amateur

    (B) durable

    (C) impartial

    (D) rental

Q17. Many of the photos you took were reproduced and _____.

(A) enlarged

(B) recorded

(C) borrowed

(D) obtained

Q18. The noise of the railroad trains keeps me _____. I can't fall asleep.

(A) delighted

(B) energetic

(C) awake

(D) sleepy

Q19. We'd better wait inside until the storm _____.

(A) isolates

(B) disturbs

(C) utilizes

(D) diminishes

Q20. While Mr. Chen was away on vacation, he allowed his mail to _____ at the mailroom.

(A) accumulate

(B) accelerate

(C) release

(D) desire

Q1. This marketing report is _____ but full of meaning.

    (A) qualified

    (B) brief

    (C) interesting

    (D) lengthy

Q2. _____ amounts of money are being invested in the local market.

    (A) Enormous

    (B) Consistent

    (C) Spacious

    (D) Advanced

Q3. My confidence slowly diminished as the _____ approached.

    (A) agreement

    (B) deadline

    (C) resource

    (D) summary

Q4. This matter is so _____ that it must not be discussed outside the office.

    (A) confidential

    (B) alarming

    (C) advanced

    (D) exciting

Q5. Comparison and contrast are often used _____ in advertisements.

(A) internationally

(B) interestingly

(C) successfully

(D) unwillingly

Q6. The PR is trying to take steps to _____ the damage.

(A) dominate

(B) elicit

(C) command

(D) minimize

Q7. All team members were surprised greatly by his _____ decision.

(A) appropriate

(B) frequent

(C) violent

(D) sudden

Q8. The factory is now trying to _____ a new product model.

(A) manufacture

(B) pay

(C) devastate

(D) distill

Q9. The cost of living in nearly every country in the world has

_____ in the past decade.

(A) appreciated

(B) skyrocketed

(C) launched

(D) influenced

Q10. As a consequence of our efforts, our team _____ the desired

results.

(A) ascertained

(B) established

(C) concealed

(D) achieved

Q11. The technology provider has _____ ten million dollars for a

new system.

(A) constituted

(B) budgeted

(C) integrated

(D) proclaimed

Q12. We are looking for a _____ to sell our software products in South America.

(A) manufacturer

(B) publisher

(C) documentary

(D) distributor

Q13. We want to _____ consumers with high incomes, who will be more likely to take holidays abroad.

(A) encourage

(B) avoid

(C) target

(D) replace

Q14. This report is based on data _____ from more than 50 countries around the world.

(A) collected

(B) announced

(C) penetrated

(D) sold

Q15. All _____ want to reach the largest market.

(A) experts

(B) advertisers

(C) spokesmen

(D) freelancers

Q16. This marketing project seems to _____ more time than we have available.

(A) manage

(B) operate

(C) decide

(D) require

Q17. Our customers _____ from primary school students to university students.

(A) separate

(B) range

(C) contain

(D) extend

Q18. Some experts predict that the business _____ will improve next year.

(A) change

(B) weather

(C) climate

(D) atmosphere

Q19. Our products are sold to customers through retailers, outlets, and other distribution _____.

(A) recipients

(B) channels

(C) conferences

(D) aspects

Q20. This marketing project is complicated and we need more time to _____ it.

(A) navigate

(B) generate

(C) compare

(D) disperse

Q1. Glassmaking is a _____ industry in the United States.

(A) sizable

(B) surprising

(C) comfortable

(D) spacious

Q2. Our manager mentioned that every effort should be made to

reduce the budget _____.

(A) purposely

(B) willingly

(C) substantially

(D) ineffectively

Q3. Many _____ gems are sold on today's market.

(A) artificial

(B) fragrant

(C) radical

(D) successful

Q4. Jenny is such a _____ business woman that she never loses

money in any transaction.

(A) trendy

(B) wealthy

(C) shrewd

(D) strong

Q5. The price of gold _____ a lot on the world market last quarter.

    (A) coincided

    (B) fluctuated

    (C) modified

    (D) generated

Q6. The writer won the prize for his _____ story.

    (A) ridiculous

    (B) pervasive

    (C) massive

    (D) exclusive

Q7. We can't always play it safe. Sometimes we need to take a _____.

    (A) debt

    (B) risk

    (C) variety

    (D) backhander

Q8. These figures reached a _____ in 2013 when over 2 million smart phones were sold.

    (A) peak

    (B) point

    (C) edition

    (D) limit

Q9. I would like to choose the bag that is more _____.

    (A) intangible

    (B) accountable

    (C) convincible

    (D) durable

Q10. Could we have a quick _____ about the sales conference?

    (A) word

    (B) sentence

    (C) speech

    (D) workshop

Q11. About half our sales are to the _____ market and half are to the industrial market.

    (A) privilege

    (B) consumer

    (C) impasse

    (D) property

Q12. I'd like you to send me your sales _____ every week instead of every month.

    (A) sessions

    (B) personnel

    (C) statistics

    (D) signatures

Q13. Please call the warehouse and check if they have more office
_____ in stock.

(A) ingredients

(B) elements

(C) supplies

(D) expenses

Q14. Our company has chosen the Japanese vendor because they
_____ the best technical service.

(A) guarantee

(B) inherit

(C) repair

(D) estimate

Q15. People who do not _____ with the company regulations will
be dismissed.

(A) prohibit

(B) comply

(C) negotiate

(D) inform

Q16. Any defective product can be returned to the reseller for a full

_____.

(A) ceremony

(B) survey

(C) refund

(D) investment

Q17. My new business is not _____ and I lose a great deal of

money.

(A) lucrative

(B) significant

(C) dwindling

(D) convenient

Q18. Our company manager has decided to hire an _____

designer to decorate the office.

(A) expectable

(B) interior

(C) outer

(D) inland

Q19. Ms. Jones decided to _____ from her position after having served for 10 years.

(A) sign

(B) recall

(C) design

(D) resign

Q20. Our long-term goal is to _____ our business to the Asia market.

(A) expand

(B) expend

(C) respond

(D) analyze

Test 7

Q1. Migrant workers have difficulty finding _____ employment.

(A) steady

(B) inspiring

(C) casual

(D) sluggish

Q2. Our employees are told to be _____ about their work.

(A) vibrant

(B) precise

(C) predictable

(D) sudden

Q3. _____ is imperative in your new job.

(A) Correction

(B) Pension

(C) Punctuality

(D) Importance

Q4. Our government implemented some _____ measures to reduce unemployment.

(A) worthless

(B) effective

(C) dynamic

(D) skeptical

Q5. I am regarded as a _____ thinker by my friends.

(A) seasoned

(B) regular

(C) deep

(D) potential

Q6. _____ business matters prevent him from taking a holiday.

(A) Urgent

(B) Handy

(C) Enough

(D) Terrifying

Q7. She gets along well with everyone, so she is the most _____ member in our team.

(A) brave

(B) congenial

(C) patient

(D) satisfied

Q8. Mr. Smith has many _____ among politicians and businessmen.

(A) acquaintances

(B) brokers

(C) administrators

(D) managers

Q9. As the president of the company, he receives an _____ salary.

(A) insufficient

(B) exploratory

(C) ample

(D) informal

Q10. If all of one's money is _____ on clothes, there may be none left to buy food or go to the movies.

(A) spending

(B) spent

(C) spender

(D) spend

Q11. Honesty is his most _____ characteristic.

(A) outstanding

(B) flexible

(C) classified

(D) useful

Q12. He is not really _____ for this position, for he doesn't have the right training.

(A) cooperative

(B) welcome

(C) fit

(D) permitted

Q13. Our manager's greatest advantage is his _____ for diligence.

(A) reputation

(B) communication

(C) credential

(D) objection

Q14. Most people are _____ to tiredness and easily make mistakes.

(A) suitable

(B) sufficient

(C) interested

(D) susceptible

Q15. Linda was _____ because she was found to be negligent in her duties.

(A) dismissed

(B) hired

(C) promoted

(D) praised

Q16. We are all deeply impressed by his _____ to other team members.

(A) completion

(B) endurance

(C) illustration

(D) devotion

Q17. All team members say Sherry is the strongest _____ for the position.

(A) candidate

(B) carrier

(C) condition

(D) counselor

Q18. The boss is _____ to all his employees.

(A) clumsy

(B) fleeting

(C) multiple

(D) arrogant

Q19. Health experts say that walking _____ strengthens the heart and lungs.

(A) energetically

(B) gracefully

(C) seriously

(D) ambiguously

Q20. Joyce's contract will be _____ at the end of this year.

(A) struggled

(B) celebrated

(C) terminated

(D) retired

Q1. The government is _____ up its efforts to finish the project on time.

(A) improving

(B) increasing

(C) speeding

(D) extending

Q2. Lack of _____ slowed up the company's progress.

(A) decoration

(B) recommendation

(C) innovation

(D) alteration

Q3. The schedule is already _____, so it cannot be changed for your personal convenience.

(A) diluted

(B) fixed

(C) promoted

(D) judged

Q4. Because the details of the project were rather _____, we decided to reject the proposal.

(A) solid

(B) clear

(C) indefinite

(D) lucrative

Q5. That matter is totally _____ to the discussion at hand.

(A) irrelevant

(B) reasonable

(C) concrete

(D) serious

Q6. Your plan is _____ to the purpose intended.

(A) possible

(B) inadequate

(C) successive

(D) repetitive

Q7. The _____ on this office building expires at the end of this year.

(A) purchase

(B) construction

(C) lease

(D) opportunity

Q8. There are two _____ solutions to this problem.

(A) feasible

(B) chaotic

(C) natural

(D) permanent

Q9. We will _____ our business on Friday and take the weekend off.

    (A) interview

    (B) renew

    (C) conclude

    (D) dismiss

Q10. No new ideas _____ during our discussion.

    (A) delivered

    (B) emerged

    (C) arrived

    (D) showed

Q11. Managers should _____ certain rules for their workers.

    (A) weave

    (B) manufacture

    (C) nominate

    (D) determine

Q12. The committee _____ people of widely different views.

    (A) comprises

    (B) compresses

    (C) complains

    (D) handles

Q13. The two companies finally reached an _____ on a legal combination.

(A) enhancement

(B) affiliation

(C) agreement

(D) affirmation

Q14. We are unable to cooperate because of the _____ between the two companies.

(A) theory

(B) outcome

(C) mission

(D) conflict

Q15. The researchers _____ numerous experiments to find the most effective materials.

(A) conducted

(B) considered

(C) concerned

(D) contacted

Q16. We have to cancel the project due to lack of _____ and manpower.

(A) obstacles

(B) funding

(C) expense

(D) topics

Q17. It is important to set our team clear _____ so we know what we are aiming for.

(A) privileges

(B) evidence

(C) occasions

(D) goals

Q18. The Internet allows us to _____ enormous amounts of information without leaving a keyboard.

(A) invent

(B) supply

(C) access

(D) respect

Q19. The chairperson _____ our attention to a large screen at the front of the conference room.

(A) separated

(B) drew

(C) created

(D) made

Q20. We are a week behind schedule, so I think we should put everyone on _____.

(A) outpace

(B) outperform

(C) overact

(D) overtime

Q1. The warranty guarantees that all _____ parts would be replaced without charge.

(A) perfect

(B) rejected

(C) unused

(D) defective

Q2. Our company's _____ is built upon fair dealing.

(A) reputation

(B) equipment

(C) location

(D) history

Q3. The directions for operating this machine are so _____ that we could not understand them.

(A) consistent

(B) essential

(C) unusual

(D) complex

Q4. I know you have the _____ to deal with difficult customers.

(A) certainty

(B) probability

(C) capability

(D) punctuality

Q5. A person who deals with the public must be _____ at all times, even when he is tired.

(A) courteous

(B) mature

(C) anxious

(D) impatient

Q6. Our office building requires _____.

(A) variation

(B) renovation

(C) selection

(D) option

Q7. The lawyer asked the newspaper to _____ their allegations.

(A) decline

(B) withdraw

(C) upgrade

(D) allocate

Q8. You should _____ these unreasonable rules.

(A) obey

(B) exchange

(C) return

(D) abolish

Q9. Some of the products have been badly _____ because of the flood.

    (A) damaged

    (B) packed

    (C) combined

    (D) realized

Q10. This type of work in considered being pretty _____.

    (A) dangerous

    (B) slippery

    (C) broken

    (D) arbitrary

Q11. We really need to find a way to _____ this problem.

    (A) display

    (B) ignore

    (C) promise

    (D) resolve

Q12. After a few hours of discussion, we finally found a happy _____.

    (A) medium

    (B) situation

    (C) petition

    (D) method

Q13. I am calling to complain about a problem I had with a member of your _____.

(A) stockholder

(B) staff

(C) client

(D) employer

Q14. I would be _____ if you could send me a catalogue.

(A) grateful

(B) encouraged

(C) similar

(D) demanding

Q15. I am really looking forward _____ you again soon.

(A) to serving

(B) to serve

(C) serving

(D) service

Q16. The company just ordered a lot of electronic _____ .

(A) patrons

(B) devices

(C) license

(D) surgery

Q17. Instead of ignoring problems, we should _____ them positively and constructively.

(A) challenge

(B) minimize

(C) approach

(D) struggle

Q18. Our manager wants all team members to _____ all gifts from suppliers, no matter how small they may be.

(A) refuse

(B) negotiate

(C) modify

(D) secure

Q19. I am _____ sorry we are late. It was difficult to find a parking space around here.

(A) randomly

(B) terribly

(C) surprisingly

(D) gradually

Q20. The suppliers _____ to deliver the equipment within five
weeks of receiving our order.

(A) designed

(B) explained

(C) guaranteed

(D) achieved

Q1. He is expected to exert the _____ influence in the industry.

    (A) negative

    (B) predominant

    (C) backward

    (D) opposing

Q2. There are some _____ in the system of operation in that organization.

    (A) defects

    (B) perfections

    (C) signatures

    (D) procedures

Q3. Home buyers are proceeding _____ because of the high interest rates.

    (A) healthily

    (B) cautiously

    (C) willingly

    (D) silently

Q4. Many businesses have turned to automation in order to produce goods more _____.

    (A) expensively

    (B) particularly

    (C) economically

    (D) simply

Q5. The strategies taken by the government failed to _____ unemployment.

(A) reduce

(B) increase

(C) require

(D) commit

Q6. These two soft-drink companies will _____ soon.

(A) organize

(B) manage

(C) merge

(D) dispute

Q7. The invention of the computer _____ business procedures.

(A) revolutionized

(B) burned

(C) disrupted

(D) declined

Q8. The employers and the strikers are at a _____.

(A) roundabout

(B) deadlock

(C) intersection

(D) development

Q9. Our company has been beaten in some markets by more sharply-focused _____, but we keep fighting.

(A) customers

(B) professors

(C) partners

(D) competitors

Q10. Good-IT Company regularly _____ 20% of its turnover in research and development.

(A) removes

(B) invests

(C) delivers

(D) entices

Q11. We are increasing our _____ of the world's beverage markets.

(A) share

(B) activity

(C) property

(D) treatment

Q12. Best-Software is active in the world markets and _____ over four thousand people worldwide.

(A) installs

(B) deploys

(C) employs

(D) relinquishes

Q13. Building team _____ is always the crucial point of what I try to do as a manager.

(A) decision

(B) crisis

(C) agenda

(D) spirit

Q14. Soft-Drink, Japan's largest drinks group, has _____ plans to lay off 500 staff redundant in Tokyo.

(A) announced

(B) motivated

(C) guided

(D) advertised

Q15. Our director, Mr. Smith, is _____ for strategic coordination.

(A) necessary

(B) rewarding

(C) professional

(D) responsible

Q16. We are going to open a new sales office in Vietnam, so we need to discuss _____.

(A) recruitment

(B) criticism

(C) recession

(D) motivation

Q17. Our company is trying to throw out _____ and develop a new company culture.

(A) tradition

(B) mission

(C) bureaucracy

(D) opportunity

Q18. Many senior managers complain that too much traveling makes them _____.

(A) friendly

(B) irritable

(C) outstanding

(D) appealing

Q19. A recent survey found that Asian executives have different
_____ to life.

(A) questions

(B) pressure

(C) subjects

(D) attitudes

Q20. Our company's activities are _____ into four business areas.

(A) divided

(B) founded

(C) dismissed

(D) compared

實力測驗詳解
Answer Key

Circumstances are the rulers of the weak,
instrument of the wise.

弱者困於環境，智者利用環境。

Q1. My name is Lily Chen. I have an _____ with Ms. Anderson at 3.

我是陳莉莉。我三點跟 Anderson 小姐有約。

(A) affirmation 證實

(B) appointment 約會

(C) excellence 完美

(D) application 應用

Q2. It's a(n) _____ to meet you, Mr. Steve.

很榮幸認識您，Steve 先生。

(A) strategy 策略

(B) opportunity 機會

(C) fortune 運氣

(D) pleasure 榮幸

Q3. Our company has its _____ in Singapore.

我們公司總部設在新加坡。

(A) rooms 房間

(B) wrinkles 皺紋

(C) beverage 飲料

(D) headquarters 總部

Q4. Our _____ product manager will speak at this conference, as the manager is on business travel.

我們的產品經理出差，因此將由副產品經理在研討會上發言。

(A) deputy 副手

(B) depressed 沮喪的

(C) domestic 國內的

(D) disnatured 不近人情的

Q5. Our manager's spacious new office _____ the city.

從我們經理的寬敞辦公室可以鳥瞰全市。

(A) overwhelmed 受衝擊的

(B) overlooked 鳥瞰

(C) overcame 克服

(D) overruled 掌控

Q6. Anna Chen's mystery novels have a _____ audience in Taiwan.

陳安娜的推理小說在台灣有廣大讀者群。

(A) developed 開發的

(B) tremendous 大量的

(C) demanding 苛求的

(D) physical 物理的

Q7. I have a _____ of miniature dolls.

我收集小型娃娃公仔。

(A) collection 收集

(B) contribution 貢獻

(C) resolution 決心

(D) promotion 升遷

Q8. The meeting will be _____ to our new product launch.

這場會議對我們的新產品上市將有所助益。

(A) interesting 有趣的

(B) deserted 遺棄的

(C) delighted 高興的

(D) conducive 有益的

Q9. The boardroom is _____ by sales department.

會議室被業務部佔用了。

(A) impressed 有印象的

(B) occupied 佔用的

(C) closed 關閉的

(D) rejected 拒絕的

Q10. After watching the sunset, I was left with a very _____ feeling.

看了夕陽後，我的心情感到很寧靜。

(A) severe 劇烈的

(B) peaceful 寧靜的

(C) sleepy 想睡的

(D) serious 嚴重的

Q11. In Taipei, people have to move quickly to _____ the cars in the streets.

在台北，人們在路上要快步行走以避開車流。

(A) process 處理

(B) dodge 躲避

(C) control 控制

(D) cause 引起

Q12. In many companies, the person who fails to collaborate well with team members is likely to be _____ by others.

在很多公司裡，無法跟團隊成員合作的人通常會被孤立。

(A) isolated 孤立

(B) preserved 保護

(C) encouraged 鼓勵

(D) promoted 升遷

Q13. I am forever _____ for your kind assistance.

我永遠感激你的熱心協助。

(A) dependent 依賴的

(B) grateful 感激的

(C) optimistic 樂觀的

(D) constant 持續的

Q14. My position on this issue is _____.

我對此議題的立場不變。

(A) casual 隨便的

(B) unusual 不尋常的

(C) punctual 準時的

(D) unchangeable 不變的

Q15. During the rainy season, we sometimes have a whole month of _____ rain.

在雨季，有時會連續下一整個月的雨。

(A) defective 有缺陷的

(B) continuous 連續的

(C) prolific 多產的

(D) violent 暴力的

Q16. George is one of my _____ relatives.

喬治是我一個遠房親戚。

(A) native 原生的

(B) realistic 現實的

(C) bloody 血紅的

(D) distant 遠親的

Q17. Lack of sleep is _____ to your health.

睡眠不足有損健康。

(A) harmful 有害的

(B) annoying 惱人的

(C) puzzling 疑惑的

(D) faithful 忠誠的

Q18. Self-confidence is a(n) _____ factor for success.

自信心是成功的必要因素。

(A) familiar 熟悉的

(B) negative 負面的

(C) essential 必要的

(D) minor 微小的

Q19. It is a mistake to _____ that riches always bring happiness.

一味認為有錢就會帶來快樂，這是不對的。

(A) suppose 假定

(B) show 顯示

(C) appear 顯露

(D) introduce 介紹

Q20. It is a fact that Mr. Hill is quite _____. It's not easy to change his mind.

的確，Hill 先生總是堅持己見。想要他改變心意還真是不容易。

(A) breakable 易破的

(B) inaccurate 不精確的

(C) tolerant 容忍的

(D) inflexible 不容改變的

Q1. I intend to discuss our XPM project and _____ a preliminary proposal for your attention.

我想討論 XPM 的案子，也附上了初步的提案給您參考。

(A) charge 索價

(B) handle 處理

(C) enclose 將（文件）封入

(D) modify 更改

Q2. If you require any further information, please do not _____ to contact me.

若您需要任何進一步的資料，歡迎隨時聯絡我。

(A) hesitate 猶豫

(B) receive 接收

(C) include 包括

(D) believe 相信

Q3. Thanks for your email asking for ways of increasing sales morale. Please find _____ document with specific plans for this.

謝謝你寄信過來詢問如何增加業務士氣。請詳見附件內文的具體計劃。

(A) attaches 附加

(B) attached 附屬的

(C) attachment 附件

(D) attaching 附加

Q4. Following our phone conversation last week, I am writing to
_____ that I can speak at next month's conference.

我們上週電話討論過後，我寫信是想確認我可以在下個月的會議
中發表演講。

(A) reform 改造

(B) transform 變換

(C) elicit 引出

(D) confirm 確認

Q5. Our company has a _____ format for writing letters to clients.

我們公司寫給客戶的信件有標準格式。

(A) standing 站立的

(B) standard 標準的

(C) standardize 標準化

(D) stands 站立

Q6. I am looking forward to your _____ response.

我期待您的即時回覆。

(A) prompt 即時的

(B) promotion 升遷

(C) previous 先前的

(D) promptly 快速地

Q7. We _____ the problem you experienced with the Z493 model.

我們很遺憾您在使用 Z493 型號產品時遭遇問題。

(A) guide 引導

(B) please 欣喜

(C) occupy 佔領

(D) regret 遺憾

Q8. I am writing to _____ our next PPM meeting to review our projects.

我寫信是要安排下一個產品績效管理會議來檢視一下我們的專案。

(A) organized 安排（動詞過去式）

(B) organize 安排（動詞一般式）

(C) organization 安排（名詞）

(D) organizing 安排（動詞進行式）

Q9. Please confirm your arrival details so that I can _____ for someone to pick you up at the airport.

請確認您的抵達細節，以便我安排人員去機場接你。

(A) finish 完成

(B) arrange 安排

(C) conduct 執行

(D) submit 呈交

Q10. Please let me know as soon as possible if these dates are

_____.

請儘速讓我知道這些日期是否可行。

(A) convenient 方便的

(B) professional 專業的

(C) standard 標準的

(D) pleasant 愉快的

Q11. This letter is to confirm your _____ at the quarterly training workshop to be held in Taipei.

此信是要確認您報名參加在台北舉辦的季度訓練會議。

(A) autonomy 自治權

(B) endorsement 贊同

(C) enrollment 報名

(D) notice 公告

Q12. Payments made after October 3rd will result in _____ fees being added to the registration fee.

十月三日之後的付款會加收逾期的額外費用。

(A) overlook 忽視

(B) overdue 過期的

(C) overwhelm 壓倒

(D) overrule 掌控

Q13. Using plain language and less _____ will make the report clearer.

為了使報告易讀易懂，要使用平實的語言，少用一些專業術語。

(A) jargon 行話

(B) credibility 可信度

(C) vocabulary 單字

(D) plan 計劃

Q14. I _____ recommend that you check the email once again before you send it out.

我強烈建議你在寄出電子郵件之前再檢查一次。

(A) fortunately 幸運地

(B) professionally 專業地

(C) sharply 急速地

(D) strongly 強烈地

Q15. With the advent of the Internet, many companies are now _____ products online.

有了網際網路之後，很多公司都在線上行銷產品。

(A) marketing 行銷

(B) making 製造

(C) progressing 進展

(D) delivering 遞送

Q16. Mr. Smith asked me to _____ to his message as soon as possible.

Smith 先生要我儘快回覆他的訊息。

(A) rewrite 改寫

(B) return 返回

(C) retrieve 取回

(D) reply 回覆

Q17. Did you have _____ to look over my report, Sherry?

Sherry，妳可以幫我看一下我的報告嗎？

(A) proof 證據

(B) chance 機會

(C) period 時期

(D) energy 精神

Q18. The _____ sales report must be finished by the end of next month.

年度業務報告要在下個月底前完成。

(A) annual 年度的

(B) frequent 經常的

(C) practical 實際的

(D) useful 有用的

Q19. We did not get the _____, because we missed the deadline.

因為我們錯過了最後期限，所以沒有拿到案子的合約。

(A) communication 溝通

(B) confirmation 確認

(C) contract 合約

(D) construction 建造

Q20. It took four workers three days to _____ the task.

這項任務要四個人花三天才做完。

(A) complete 完成

(B) accommodate 容納

(C) approve 准許

(D) compare 比較

Test 3

Q1. Can you put me through to _____ 333, please?

麻煩幫我轉接到分機 333，謝謝。

(A) extension 分機

(B) expansion 擴充

(C) expiration 到期

(D) exterior 外部的

Q2. We must have a bad connection because I keep hearing an _____ on the line.

我們通話品質不好，因為我一直聽到線上的回音。

(A) attention 注意

(B) echo 回聲

(C) objective 目標

(D) urgency 緊急

Q3. Is there anything else we need to discuss _____ our project?

還有任何專案相關的事需要討論嗎？

(A) rearrange 重新安排

(B) reorganize 改組

(C) retrieve 取回

(D) regarding 關於

Q4. Could you please give Mr. Thomson a _____ for me when he gets in?

麻煩你在 Thomson 先生進來後，告訴他我的留言。

(A) mirage 海市蜃樓

(B) message 訊息，留言

(C) massage 按摩

(D) marriage 婚姻

Q5. My assistance called the airline to _____ my tickets.

我的助理打電話給航空公司核對機票訂位事宜。

(A) verification 證實（名詞）

(B) verify 核對（動詞一般式）

(C) verified 核對（動詞過去式）

(D) verifying 核對（動詞進行式）

Q6. I'm afraid you've reached the wrong department. I'll _____ you back to the operator.

你恐怕是找錯部門了。我幫你轉回總機。

(A) call 打電話

(B) service 服務

(C) transfer 轉接

(D) change 改變

Q7. You can reach marketing department by _____ "7".

若要接行銷部，請現在按 "7"。

(A) writing 書寫

(B) submitting 送出

(C) talking 談話

(D) dialing 撥號

Q8. Due to a _____ problem, the office phones won't be working for the next 20 minutes.

由於出現技術問題，接下來的 20 分鐘辦公室的電話將無法使用。

(A) technical 技術性的

(B) noisy 吵雜的

(C) thorough 完全的

(D) wonderful 美好的

Q9. After you arrive, just ask for Ms. Wilson at the _____ desk.

你抵達之後，就到接待處找 Wilson 小姐。

(A) employee 員工

(B) reception 接待

(C) office 辦公室

(D) assistance 協助

Q10. Please tell him it is _____ that he calls me back before noon.

請告知他這很重要，要在中午前回我電話。

(A) essential 重要的

(B) aggressive 積極的

(C) polite 禮貌的

(D) complex 複雜的

Q11. Your report only has a few _____ statements.

你的報告內僅有幾處敘述不夠清楚。

(A) ambiguous 含糊不清的

(B) impossible 不可能的

(C) necessary 有需要的

(D) reimburse 償還

Q12. My boss handed me an _____ before my day off.

我的老闆在我休假日前指派給我一項工作。

(A) assignment 工作

(B) admission 許可

(C) extension 延期

(D) indication 指示

Q13. The time of the interview is not _____ for me.

這個面談時間我無法配合。

(A) fortunate 幸運的

(B) polite 有禮貌的

(C) appropriate 恰當的

(D) useful 有用的

Q14. Mary is a very _____ person to work with.

瑪莉是一個很好相處的工作夥伴。

(A) forgetful 健忘的

(B) agreeable 討人喜歡的

(C) elderly 年老的

(D) generous 慷慨的

Q15. Mr. Jones' factory _____ us with raw materials.

Jones 先生的工廠供應我們原物料。

(A) disturbs 妨礙

(B) supplies 供應

(C) responds 回應

(D) reflects 反映

Q16. Are you familiar with the _____ for purchasing stationery?

你對採購文具的程序熟悉嗎？

(A) procedure 程序

(B) donation 捐獻

(C) harmony 和諧

(D) ambiance 氣氛

Q17. Tom follows orders well, but he seldom _____ action.

湯姆懂得遵循命令，但他鮮少主動行事。

(A) urges 催促

(B) expresses 表達

(C) initiates 開始

(D) implies 暗示

Q18. This factory _____ 3,000 laptops a month.

這家工廠每月生產三千台筆記型電腦。

(A) produces 生產

(B) pushes 推

(C) plans 計劃

(D) bakes 烘烤

Q19. I will send you a _____ of the document.

我會寄給你一份此文件的複本。

(A) purchase 購買

(B) category 類別

(C) duplicate 複本

(D) permission 許可

Q20. This _____ analysis supported my points.

這份關鍵性的分析證實了我的觀點。

(A) conservative 保守的

(B) critical 關鍵的

(C) realistic 現實的

(D) overdue 過期的

Q1. After working for two hours, Alice spent the _____ of the afternoon relaxing.

Alice 下午工作兩小時之後，其餘時間都在休閒。

(A) pastime 娛樂

(B) minority 少數

(C) remainder 剩餘

(D) balance 平衡

Q2. He _____ a car accident due to his quick reflexes.

由於他的反應快速，避免了一場車禍。

(A) produced 生產

(B) happened 發生

(C) caused 引發

(D) prevented 預防

Q3. The _____ of the gigantic hotel began last year.

這間大型飯店從去年開始建造。

(A) intersection 交叉路口

(B) construction 建造

(C) circulation 流通

(D) duration 期間

Q4. As a result of the expansion of the public transportation system, our company will _____ our shuttle bus service.

大眾運輸系統擴建了之後，我們公司便不再提供接駁車的服務。

(A) celebrate 慶祝

(B) emerge 出現

(C) discontinue 中止

(D) complete 完成

Q5. The _____ left the town in complete disorder.

颶風讓這個村落變得滿目瘡痍。

(A) hurricane 颶風

(B) guidance 指導

(C) insurance 保險

(D) content 內容

Q6. The company aims at making _____ products.

這間公司致力於製造創新的產品。

(A) disperse 散發

(B) bustling 繁忙的

(C) dramatic 戲劇性的

(D) innovative 創新的

Q7. Henry has been working _____ for decades.

Henry 已經在海外工作數十年了。

(A) overseas 在海外

(B) concisely 簡潔地

(C) outright 徹底地

(D) hereby 藉此

Q8. The lake _____ in the middle of the park is calm today.

位於公園中央的湖，水面很平靜。

(A) satisfied 滿足的

(B) situated 位於…的

(C) evaluated 估價的

(D) bounded 有界限的

Q9. The caterers must know _____ how many people are expected.

宴會承辦人必須知道會出席的大概人數。

(A) approximately 大約地

(B) confidentially 機密地

(C) similarly 相似地

(D) separately 分別地

Q10. The building was _____ within a very short time.

此棟樓在很短時間內就被清空了。

(A) evacuated 疏散

(B) authorized 授權

(C) displayed 展示

(D) liberated 解放

Q11. People who live in that developed country enjoy a(n) _____ lifestyle.

那個已開發國家的人們過著奢華的生活。

(A) complicated 複雜的

(B) impractical 不切實際的

(C) deluxe 豪華的

(D) difficult 困難的

Q12. It took me five hours to reach the _____ in such a rainy day.

在這樣的下雨天，我花了五個小時才到達目的地。

(A) destination 目的地

(B) appreciation 欣賞

(C) reservation 預訂

(D) conclusion 結論

Q13. Miss Lu _____ that her car was hit by a van.

呂小姐聲稱她的車是被一台小貨車撞上。

(A) entices 引誘

(B) softens 軟化

(C) claims 聲稱

(D) cancels 取消

Q14. We had a lovely visit because the Jones was so _____.

瓊斯一家人招待周到，我們玩得非常開心。

(A) rude 粗魯的

(B) hospitable 好客殷勤的

(C) tolerable 可容忍的

(D) confusing 混淆的

Q15. Shy people are often _____ at parties and other social gatherings.

害羞的人在派對或其他社交場合中通常不被注意。

(A) overlooked 忽略

(B) overrated 高估

(C) overseen 監視

(D) overtaken 追趕

Q16. Last night I went to a concert given by a group of _____ musicians.

昨晚我參加了一場由業餘音樂家所舉辦的音樂會。

(A) amateur 業餘的

(B) durable 耐用的

(C) impartial 客觀的

(D) rental 出租的

Q17. Many of the photos you took were reproduced and _____.

你拍的很多照片都有加洗和放大。

(A) enlarged 放大

(B) recorded 記錄

(C) borrowed 借入

(D) obtained 獲得

Q18. The noise of the railroad trains keeps me _____. I can't fall asleep.

火車的噪音讓我一直清醒著，無法入眠。

(A) delighted 快樂的

(B) energetic 精神奕奕的

(C) awake 清醒的

(D) sleepy 想睡的

Answer Key

Q19. We'd better wait inside until the storm _____.

我們最好在裡面等，直到暴風雨變小。

(A) isolates 孤立

(B) disturbs 打擾

(C) utilizes 利用

(D) diminishes 減緩

Q20. While Mr. Chen was away on vacation, he allowed his mail to

_____ at the mailroom.

陳先生渡假期間，他就讓郵件都堆在收發室。

(A) accumulate 累積

(B) accelerate 加速

(C) release 釋放

(D) desire 渴求

Q1. This marketing report is _____ but full of meaning.

這份行銷報告言簡意賅。

(A) qualified 夠資格的

(B) brief 簡略的

(C) interesting 有趣的

(D) lengthy 冗長的

Q2. _____ amounts of money are being invested in the local market.

大量資金都被投入到地方市場上。

(A) Enormous 大量的

(B) Cansistent 一致的

(C) Spacious 寬廣的

(D) Advanced 先進的

Q3. My confidence slowly diminished as the _____ approached.

隨著期限的逼近，我的信心逐漸減少。

(A) agreement 協議

(B) deadline 期限

(C) resource 資源

(D) summary 總結

Q4. This matter is so _____ that it must not be discussed outside the office.

這件事非常機密，禁止在辦公室以外討論。

(A) confidential 機密的

(B) alarming 告急的

(C) advanced 先進的

(D) exciting 令人興奮的

Q5. Comparison and contrast are often used _____ in advertisements.

比較和對比成功地被運用在廣告上。

(A) internationally 國際地

(B) interestingly 有趣地

(C) successfully 成功地

(D) unwillingly 不情願地

Q6. The PR is trying to take steps to _____ the damage.

公關部門正試著採取措施，使傷害降到最低。

(A) dominate 支配

(B) elicit 引出

(C) command 命令

(D) minimize 減到最少

Q7. All team members were surprised greatly by his _____ decision.

所有的團隊成員都對他的突然決定感到吃驚不已。

(A) appropriate 適當的

(B) frequent 頻繁的

(C) violent 暴力的

(D) sudden 突然的

Q8. The factory is now trying to _____ a new product model.

這家工廠嘗試要製作新產品的原型。

(A) manufacture 製造

(B) pay 付款

(C) devastate 毀壞

(D) distill 提煉

Q9. The cost of living in nearly every country in the world has _____ in the past decade.

過去十年，幾乎全世界每個國家的生活費都飆升許多。

(A) appreciated 感激

(B) skyrocketed 飆高

(C) launched 上市

(D) influenced 影響

Q10. As a consequence of our efforts, our team _____ the desired results.

由於大夥的努力付出，我們達成想要的結果了。

(A) ascertained 確定

(B) established 建立

(C) concealed 隱藏

(D) achieved 達成

Q11. The technology provider has _____ ten million dollars for a new system.

技術供應商為新系統編列了一千萬的預算。

(A) constituted 組成

(B) budgeted 編列預算

(C) integrated 整合

(D) proclaimed 宣佈

Q12. We are looking for a _____ to sell our software products in South America.

我們正在找可以幫我們在南美洲銷售軟體的代理商。

(A) manufacturer 製造商

(B) publisher 出版商

(C) documentary 文件

(D) distributor 代理商

Q13. We want to _____ consumers with high incomes, who will be
more likely to take holidays abroad.

我們想主攻高收入的客戶群，他們較有可能出國旅遊。

(A) encourage 鼓勵

(B) avoid 避免

(C) target 設目標於…

(D) replace 取代

Q14. This report is based on data _____ from more than 50
countries around the world.

這份報告內容來自全球五十個以上國家收集而來的資訊。

(A) collected 收集

(B) announced 宣佈

(C) penetrated 滲透

(D) sold 販賣

Q15. All _____ want to reach the largest market.

所有的廣告主都希望接觸到最多的客戶。

(A) experts 專家

(B) advertisers 廣告主

(C) spokesmen 發言人

(D) freelancers 自由作家

Q16. This marketing project seems to _____ more time than we
have available.

這個行銷專案看來會需要比我們可運用的時間更長。

(A) manage 管理

(B) operate 營運

(C) decide 決定

(D) require 要求

Q17. Our customers _____ from primary school students to
university students.

我們的目標客群範圍包括小學生到大學生。

(A) separate 分割

(B) range 範圍

(C) contain 內含

(D) extend 延伸

Q18. Some experts predict that the business _____ will improve
next year.

一些專家預測明年業務狀況會好轉。

(A) change 改變

(B) weather 天氣

(C) climate 趨勢

(D) atmosphere 氣氛

Q19. Our products are sold to customers through retailers, outlets, and other distribution _____.

我們的產品從經銷商、賣場和其他銷售管道販賣給客戶。

(A) recipients 領受人

(B) channels 管道

(C) conferences 會議

(D) aspects 觀點

Q20. This marketing project is complicated and we need more time to _____ it.

這個行銷專案很複雜，因此我們需要更多時間來運作。

(A) navigate 操控

(B) generate 產生

(C) compare 比較

(D) disperse 散播

Q1. Glassmaking is a _____ industry in the United States.

玻璃製造在美國是相當龐大的產業。

(A) sizable 相當大的

(B) surprising 驚訝的

(C) comfortable 舒適的

(D) spacious 寬敞的

Q2. Our manager mentioned that every effort should be made to reduce the budget _____.

我們經理指示,要盡力地大幅減預算。

(A) purposely 有目的地

(B) willingly 樂意地

(C) substantially 相當多地

(D) ineffectively 沒效果地

Q3. Many _____ gems are sold on today's market.

現今市面上販售很多人造珠寶。

(A) artificial 人造的

(B) fragrant 芬芳的

(C) radical 基本的

(D) successful 成功的

Q4. Jenny is such a _____ business woman that she never loses money in any transaction.

珍妮是一個很精明的生意人，她交易從未賠錢。

(A) trendy 時髦的

(B) wealthy 富有的

(C) shrewd 精明的

(D) strong 強壯的

Q5. The price of gold _____ a lot on the world market last quarter.

上一季國際市場的金價有很大的波動。

(A) coincided 符合

(B) fluctuated 波動

(C) modified 修正

(D) generated 產生

Q6. The writer won the prize for his _____ story.

那位作家靠著他的獨家故事而獲獎。

(A) ridiculous 荒謬的

(B) pervasive 普遍的

(C) massive 巨大的

(D) exclusive 獨家的

Q7. We can't always play it safe. Sometimes we need to take a

_____ .

我們不能總是保守行事。有時候冒險一下也是有必要的。

(A) debt 債

(B) risk 風險

(C) variety 多樣性

(D) backhander 賄賂

Q8. These figures reached a _____ in 2013 when over 2 million

smart phones were sold.

我們在 2013 年銷售超過兩百萬支智慧型手機，業績數字達到最

高點。

(A) peak 高峰

(B) point 要點

(C) edition 版本

(D) limit 限制

Q9. I would like to choose the bag that is more _____ .

我想選比較耐用的那個手提包。

(A) intangible 無形的

(B) accountable 應負責任的

(C) convincible 可說服的

(D) durable 耐用的

373

Q10. Could we have a quick _____ about the sales conference?

我們可以針對業務會議的事很快地討論一下嗎？

(A) word 談話

(B) sentence 句子

(C) speech 演說

(D) workshop 專題研討會

Q11. About half our sales are to the _____ market and half are to the industrial market.

我們的銷售業務在消費者市場和企業市場各佔一半。

(A) privilege 特權

(B) consumer 消費者

(C) impasse 僵局

(D) property 資產

Q12. I'd like you to send me your sales _____ every week instead of every month.

請你們每週寄業務報表給我，而非每個月寄。

(A) sessions 會議

(B) personnel 人員

(C) statistics 統計數字

(D) signatures 簽名

Q13. Please call the warehouse and check if they have more office

_____ in stock.

請打電話到倉庫去確認他們是否有辦公用品的庫存。

(A) ingredients 成份

(B) elements 要素

(C) supplies 用品

(D) expenses 經費

Q14. Our company has chosen the Japanese vendor because they

_____ the best technical service.

我們公司選擇了日本的供應商，因為他們保證提供最佳的技術服
務。

(A) guarantee 保證

(B) inherit 繼承

(C) repair 修理

(D) estimate 估計

Q15. People who do not _____ with the company regulations will

be dismissed.

沒有按照公司規定行事的人會被資遣。

(A) prohibit 禁止

(B) comply 配合

(C) negotiate 談判

(D) inform 通知

Q16. Any defective product can be returned to the reseller for a full

_____.

任何有缺陷的產品可以退給經銷商，並辦理全額退款。

(A) ceremony 典禮

(B) survey 調查

(C) refund 退費

(D) investment 投資

Q17. My new business is not _____ and I lose a great deal of money.

我的新公司沒賺錢，我還賠了很多錢。

(A) lucrative 有利可圖的

(B) significant 顯著的

(C) dwindling 日漸減少的

(D) convenient 方便的

Q18. Our company manager has decided to hire an _____ designer to decorate the office.

我們公司經理決定要請一位室內設計師來裝潢辦公室。

(A) expectable 可預期的

(B) interior 內部的

(C) outer 外面的

(D) inland 內陸的

Q19. Ms. Jones decided to _____ from her position after having served for 10 years.

Jones 小姐在服務十年之後決定辭去職務。

(A) sign 簽署

(B) recall 回想

(C) design 設計

(D) resign 辭職

Q20. Our long-term goal is to _____ our business to the Asia market.

我們的長期目標是拓展業務到亞洲市場。

(A) expand 拓展

(B) expend 花費

(C) respond 回應

(D) analyze 分析

Q1. Migrant workers have difficulty finding _____ employment.

流動勞工很難找到穩定的工作。

(A) steady 穩定的

(B) inspiring 激勵的

(C) casual 非正式的

(D) sluggish 遲緩的

Q2. Our employees are told to be _____ about their work.

我們的員工被要求工作要精準。

(A) vibrant 鮮明的

(B) precise 精確的

(C) predictable 可預料的

(D) sudden 突然的

Q3. _____ is imperative in your new job.

你的這份新工作，準時是絕對必要的。

(A) Correction 修正

(B) Pension 退休金

(C) Punctuality 準時

(D) Importance 重要性

Q4. Our government implemented some _____ measures to reduce unemployment.

政府採取了一些有效的方法來降低失業率。

(A) worthless 無價值的

(B) effective 有效的

(C) dynamic 動態的

(D) skeptical 懷疑的

Q5. I am regarded as a _____ thinker by my friends.

我朋友認為我是一個深入思考的人。

(A) seasoned 經驗豐富的

(B) regular 規律的

(C) deep 深入的

(D) potential 潛在的

Q6. _____ business matters prevent him from taking a holiday.

業務的緊急狀況導致他無法休假。

(A) Urgent 緊急的

(B) Handy 便利的

(C) Enough 足夠的

(D) Terrifying 嚇人的

Q7. She gets along well with everyone, so she is the most _____ member in our team.

她跟每個人都相處得很好，所以她在團體中人緣最好。

(A) brave 勇敢的

(B) congenial 意氣相投的

(C) patient 耐心的

(D) satisfied 滿意的

Q8. Mr. Smith has many _____ among politicians and businessmen.

Smith 先生在政商界都有熟識的朋友。

(A) acquaintances 熟識的人

(B) brokers 經紀人

(C) administrators 行政人員

(D) managers 經理

Q9. As the president of the company, he receives an _____ salary.

身為公司總裁，他支領高薪。

(A) insufficient 不足的

(B) exploratory 探險的

(C) ample 充裕的

(D) informal 非正式的

Q10. If all of one's money is _____ on clothes, there may be none left to buy food or go to the movies.

若一個人將所有的錢都花在買衣服上，那麼就可能沒有錢買食物或看電影了。

(A) spending 花費（進行式）

(B) spent 花費（被動式）

(C) spender 揮金如土的人

(D) spend 花費（動詞原形）

Q11. Honesty is his most _____ characteristic.

誠實是他最大的特色。

(A) outstanding 突出的

(B) flexible 靈活的

(C) classified 分類的

(D) useful 有用的

Q12. He is not really _____ for this position, for he doesn't have the right training.

他沒受過正統的訓練，因此不太適合這個職位。

(A) cooperative 合作的

(B) welcome 歡迎的

(C) fit 合適的

(D) permitted 准許的

Q13. Our manager's greatest advantage is his _____ for diligence.

我們經理最大的優勢就是他勤奮的好名聲。

(A) reputation 名聲

(B) communication 溝通

(C) credential 憑證

(D) objection 反對

Q14. Most people are _____ to tiredness and easily make mistakes.

大多數人在疲勞時較容易犯錯。

(A) suitable 合適的

(B) sufficient 足夠的

(C) interested 有興趣的

(D) susceptible 易受影響的

Q15. Linda was _____ because she was found to be negligent in her duties.

琳達工作粗心大意，因此被解雇了。

(A) dismissed 解雇

(B) hired 聘任

(C) promoted 升遷

(D) praised 讚許

Q16. We are all deeply impressed by his _____ to other team members.

他對其他團隊成員的貢獻讓我們印象深刻。

(A) completion 完整

(B) endurance 忍耐

(C) illustration 圖解

(D) devotion 奉獻

Q17. All team members say Sherry is the strongest _____ for the position.

所有團隊成員都認為雪莉是這個職位的最佳候選人。

(A) candidate 候選人

(B) carrier 運送者

(C) condition 條件

(D) counselor 顧問

Q18. The boss is _____ to all his employees.

那個老闆對員工表現傲慢。

(A) clumsy 笨拙的

(B) fleeting 短暫的

(C) multiple 多樣的

(D) arrogant 傲慢的

Q19. Health experts say that walking _____ strengthens the heart and lungs.

健康專家指出健走有助於強健心肺。

(A) energetically 精力充沛地

(B) gracefully 優雅地

(C) seriously 嚴肅地

(D) ambiguously 不明確地

Q20. Joyce's contract will be _____ at the end of this year.

Joyce 的合約到今年底會終止。

(A) struggled 掙扎

(B) celebrated 慶祝

(C) terminated 終止

(D) retired 退休

Q1. The government is _____ up its efforts to finish the project on time.

政府正加快腳步以如期完成專案。

(A) improving 進步

(B) increasing 增加

(C) speeding 加速

(D) extending 延長

Q2. Lack of _____ slowed up the company's progress.

缺乏創新讓公司無法進步。

(A) decoration 裝潢

(B) recommendation 推薦

(C) innovation 創新

(D) alteration 修改

Q3. The schedule is already _____, so it cannot be changed for your personal convenience.

行程已經確定，不會為了你個人的方便而改變。

(A) diluted 稀釋的

(B) fixed 固定的

(C) promoted 升遷

(D) judged 評定

Q4. Because the details of the project were rather _____, we decided to reject the proposal.

本專案的細節都很模擬兩可，因此我們決定要推翻這個提案。

(A) solid 堅固的

(B) clear 清楚的

(C) indefinite 模糊的

(D) lucrative 有利可圖的

Q5. That matter is totally _____ to the discussion at hand.

此事和我們目前在討論的事完全無關。

(A) irrelevant 無關的

(B) reasonable 合理的

(C) concrete 具體的

(D) serious 嚴重的

Q6. Your plan is _____ to the purpose intended.

你的計劃並不能達成我們想要的結果。

(A) possible 可能的

(B) inadequate 不夠的

(C) successive 連續的

(D) repetitive 重複的

Q7. The _____ on this office building expires at the end of this year.

這棟辦公大樓的租約到年底到期。

(A) purchase 購買

(B) construction 建築

(C) lease 租約

(D) opportunity 機會

Q8. There are two _____ solutions to this problem.

針對此問題有兩個可行的解決方案。

(A) feasible 可行的

(B) chaotic 混亂的

(C) natural 自然的

(D) permanent 永久的

Q9. We will _____ our business on Friday and take the weekend off.

我們會在週五結束公務，然後週末休息。

(A) interview 面談

(B) renew 更新

(C) conclude 結束

(D) dismiss 解散

Q10. No new ideas _____ during our discussion.

我們的討論中沒有新的想法出現。

(A) delivered 運送

(B) emerged 顯露

(C) arrived 到達

(D) showed 展現

Q11. Managers should _____ certain rules for their workers.

經理應該為底下的員工確立一些規定。

(A) weave 編織

(B) manufacture 製造

(C) nominate 提名

(D) determine 確立

Q12. The committee _____ people of widely different views.

此委員會是由不同觀點的人所組成的。

(A) comprises 構成

(B) compresses 壓縮

(C) complains 抱怨

(D) handles 處理

Q13. The two companies finally reached an _____ on a legal combination.

那兩家公司終於對合併案達成了共識。

(A) enhancement 增強

(B) affiliation 入會

(C) agreement 同意

(D) affirmation 證實

Q14. We are unable to cooperate because of the _____ between the two companies.

因為兩家公司之間的衝突，使我們無法合作。

(A) theory 理論

(B) outcome 結果

(C) mission 任務

(D) conflict 衝突

Q15. The researchers _____ numerous experiments to find the most effective materials.

研發人員要進行各種實驗，以找出效果最佳的材質。

(A) conducted 實施

(B) considered 考慮

(C) concerned 憂慮

(D) contacted 接觸

Q16. We have to cancel the project due to lack of _____ and manpower.

因為缺乏資金和人力，我們必須取消這個專案。

(A) obstacles 阻礙

(B) funding 資金

(C) expense 花費

(D) topics 主題

Q17. It is important to set our team clear _____ so we know what we are aiming for.

為團隊設立清楚的目標是很重要的，這樣我們才知道努力的方向。

(A) privileges 特權

(B) evidence 證據

(C) occasions 場合

(D) goals 目標

Q18. The Internet allows us to _____ enormous amounts of information without leaving a keyboard.

網際網路讓我們只用鍵盤就可以取得大量的資訊。

(A) invent 投資

(B) supply 提供

(C) access 取得

(D) respect 尊重

Q19. The chairperson _____ our attention to a large screen at the front of the conference room.

主席把我們的注意力引到會議室前方的大螢幕上。

(A) separated 分開

(B) drew 吸引

(C) created 創造

(D) made 做

Q20. We are a week behind schedule, so I think we should put everyone on _____.

我們的進度已經落後一週了，我認為我們應要求所有員工加班。

(A) outpace 趕過

(B) outperform 勝過

(C) overact 誇張行事

(D) overtime 超時

Q1. The warranty guarantees that all _____ parts would be replaced without charge.

保證書上擔保所有的瑕疵零件都可以免費更換。

(A) perfect 完美的

(B) rejected 拒絕的

(C) unused 沒使用的

(D) defective 有缺陷的

Q2. Our company's _____ is built upon fair dealing.

我們公司的名聲是建構在公平交易的基礎上。

(A) reputation 名聲

(B) equipment 設備

(C) location 地點

(D) history 歷史

Q3. The directions for operating this machine are so _____ that we could not understand them.

操作機器的指示太複雜，我們無法理解。

(A) consistent 一致的

(B) essential 必要的

(C) unusual 奇特的

(D) complex 複雜的

Q4. I know you have the _____ to deal with difficult customers.

我知道你有處理難纏客戶的能力。

(A) certainty 確定性

(B) probability 可能性

(C) capability 能力

(D) punctuality 守時

Q5. A person who deals with the public must be _____ at all

times, even when he is tired.

跟群眾打交道的人，就算累了也要隨時保持彬彬有禮。

(A) courteous 謙恭有禮的

(B) mature 成熟的

(C) anxious 焦慮的

(D) impatient 不耐煩的

Q6. Our office building requires _____.

我們的辦公大樓需要整修。

(A) variation 變化

(B) renovation 裝修

(C) selection 選擇

(D) option 選項

Q7. The lawyer asked the newspaper to _____ their allegations.

律師要求這家報社收回他們的聲明。

(A) decline 回絕

(B) withdraw 收回

(C) upgrade 升級

(D) allocate 分配

Q8. You should _____ these unreasonable rules.

你應該要廢除不合理的規定。

(A) obey 遵從

(B) exchange 交換

(C) return 回歸

(D) abolish 廢止

Q9. Some of the products have been badly _____ because of the flood.

有些產品因為淹水受到嚴重的破壞。

(A) damaged 破壞

(B) packed 包裝

(C) combined 結合

(D) realized 瞭解

Q10. This type of work in considered being pretty _____.

這種工作被認為是頗具危險性的。

(A) dangerous 危險的

(B) slippery 滑的

(C) broken 破碎的

(D) arbitrary 武斷的

Q11. We really need to find a way to _____ this problem.

我們的確需要找個辦法來解決這個問題。

(A) display 顯示

(B) ignore 忽略

(C) promise 答應

(D) resolve 解決

Q12. After a few hours of discussion, we finally found a happy

_____.

經過數個小時的討論，我們終於找到折衷的辦法了。

(A) medium 中間

(B) situation 情況

(C) petition 申訴

(D) method 方法

Q13. I am calling to complain about a problem I had with a member of your _____.

我打電話的目的是要抱怨你們公司的某位員工。

(A) stockholder 股東

(B) staff 員工

(C) client 客戶

(D) employer 雇主

Q14. I would be _____ if you could send me a catalogue.

若您可以寄一本目錄給我，那就再好不過了。

(A) grateful 欣喜的

(B) encouraged 受激勵的

(C) similar 類似的

(D) demanding 苛求的

Q15. I am really looking forward _____ you again soon.

我很期待再次為您服務。

(A) to serving 服務

(B) to serve 服務

(C) serving 服務（動名詞）

(D) service 服務（名詞）

Q16. The company just ordered a lot of electronic _____ .

那間公司剛剛訂購了許多電子儀器。

(A) patrons 顧客

(B) devices 儀器

(C) license 許可

(D) surgery 手術

Q17. Instead of ignoring problems, we should _____ them

positively and constructively.

與其忽視問題的存在,我們應該積極面對問題並有效地解決。

(A) challenge 挑戰

(B) minimize 減至最低

(C) approach 著手處理

(D) struggle 掙扎

Q18. Our manager wants all team members to _____ all gifts from

suppliers, no matter how small they may be.

我們經理要求所有團隊成員都不能收受廠商的贈禮,不管禮品多

小都不能收。

(A) refuse 拒絕

(B) negotiate 談判

(C) modify 修改

(D) secure 獲得

Q19. I am _____ sorry we are late. It was difficult to find a parking space around here.

非常抱歉我們遲到了。這附近的停車位有點難找。

(A) randomly 任意地

(B) terribly 非常地

(C) surprisingly 訝異地

(D) gradually 逐漸地

Q20. The suppliers _____ to deliver the equipment within five weeks of receiving our order.

供應商保證在收到訂單後的五週內會運送設備過來。

(A) designed 設計

(B) explained 解釋

(C) guaranteed 保證

(D) achieved 達成

Q1. He is expected to exert the _____ influence in the industry.

大家預期他會在業界發揮顯著的影響。

(A) negative 負面的

(B) predominant 佔支配地位的

(C) backward 落後的

(D) opposing 反對的

Q2. There are some _____ in the system of operation in that organization.

那家企業的營運系統有瑕疵。

(A) defects 缺陷

(B) perfections 完美

(C) signatures 簽名

(D) procedures 步驟

Q3. Home buyers are proceeding _____ because of the high interest rates.

高貸款利率讓買房者都小心謹慎。

(A) healthily 健康地

(B) cautiously 謹慎地

(C) willingly 願意地

(D) silently 沉默地

Q4. Many businesses have turned to automation in order to produce goods more _____.

很多企業都將生產型態轉為自動化，以用更經濟的方式製造產品。

(A) expensively 昂貴地

(B) particularly 特定地

(C) economically 節省地

(D) simply 簡易地

Q5. The strategies taken by the government failed to _____ unemployment.

政府為降低失業率所採取的策略並未奏效。

(A) reduce 降低

(B) increase 增加

(C) require 需要

(D) commit 做出

Q6. These two soft-drink companies will _____ soon.

這兩家軟性飲料公司即將合併。

(A) organize 安排

(B) manage 管理

(C) merge 合併

(D) dispute 爭論

Q7. The invention of the computer _____ business procedures.

電腦的發明徹底地改變了商業流程。

(A) revolutionized 改革

(B) burned 燒毀

(C) disrupted 混亂

(D) declined 降低

Q8. The employers and the strikers are at a _____.

資方和罷工者陷入了僵局。

(A) roundabout 圓環

(B) deadlock 僵局

(C) intersection 十字路口

(D) development 發展

Q9. Our company has been beaten in some markets by more sharply-focused _____, but we keep fighting.

我們公司在某些市場被更強勢的競爭對手打壓，但我們持續反擊。

(A) customers 客戶

(B) professors 教授

(C) partners 合作夥伴

(D) competitors 競爭對手

Q10. Good-IT Company regularly _____ 20% of its turnover in research and development.

「優網公司」定期將營業額的 20% 投資在研發上。

(A) removes 移動

(B) invests 投資

(C) delivers 寄送

(D) entices 誘使

Q11. We are increasing our _____ of the world's beverage markets.

我們正在提高在全球飲料市場的佔有率。

(A) share 市佔率

(B) activity 活動

(C) property 財產

(D) treatment 處理

Q12. Best-Software is active in the world markets and _____ over four thousand people worldwide.

「最佳軟體公司」在全球市場很活躍,並雇用了超過四千位員工。

(A) installs 安裝

(B) deploys 部署

(C) employs 聘用

(D) relinquishes 放棄

Q13. Building team _____ is always the crucial point of what I try

to do as a manager.

身為經理人，建立起團隊精神是我的重要目標之一。

(A) decision 決定

(B) crisis 危機

(C) agenda 議程

(D) spirit 精神

Q14. Soft-Drink, Japan's largest drinks group, has _____ plans to

lay off 500 staff redundant in Tokyo.

日本的最大飲料集團「軟性飲料」，宣佈公司計畫要裁撤東京辦

公室的五百個員工。

(A) announced 宣佈

(B) motivated 激勵

(C) guided 引導

(D) advertised 刊登廣告

Q15. Our director, Mr. Smith, is _____ for strategic coordination.

我們的主管 Smith 先生，負責的是策略協調。

(A) necessary 必須的

(B) rewarding 有益的

(C) professional 專業的

(D) responsible 負責的

Q16. We are going to open a new sales office in Vietnam, so we need to discuss _____.

我們即將在越南開設新的業務處，因此我們要討論員工的招募。

(A) recruitment 招募

(B) criticism 批評

(C) recession 衰退

(D) motivation 動機

Q17. Our company is trying to throw out _____ and develop a new company culture.

我們公司試著擺脫官僚作風並發展新的企業文化。

(A) tradition 傳統

(B) mission 使命

(C) bureaucracy 官僚

(D) opportunity 機會

Q18. Many senior managers complain that too much traveling makes them _____.

很多資深經理人抱怨出差太頻繁讓他們感到煩躁。

(A) friendly 友善的

(B) irritable 煩躁的

(C) outstanding 突出的

(D) appealing 迷人的

Q19. A recent survey found that Asian executives have different
_____ to life.

最近一份研究發現，亞洲地區的執行長對生活抱持不同態度。

(A) questions 問題

(B) pressure 壓力

(C) subjects 主題

(D) attitudes 態度

Q20. Our company's activities are _____ into four business areas.

我們公司的業務分成四個領域。

(A) divided 區分

(B) founded 建立

(C) dismissed 解散

(D) compared 比較

Notes

國家圖書館出版品預行編目資料

新多益黃金單字／文之勤著. -- 初版. -- 臺北市：師德文
教, 2014.08
　　面；　　公分
　ISBN 978-986-6915-61-1（平裝附光碟）

　1. 多益測驗　　2. 詞彙

805. 1895　　　　　　　　　　　　　103013242

考前準備系列　TP201

新多益黃金單字

出版及發行／師德文教股份有限公司
台北市忠孝西路一段 100 號 12 樓
TEL: (02) 2382-0961　FAX: (02) 2382-0841
http://www.cet-taiwan.com

發 行 人／陳文棋

作　　者／文之勤

總 編 輯／邱靖媛

執行編輯／孟慶蓉

文字編輯／王清雪

封面設計／林雅蓁

美術編輯／林淑慧

總經銷／紅螞蟻圖書有限公司
台北市內湖區舊宗路二段121巷19號
TEL:(02) 2795-3656　Fax:(02) 2795-4100
特約門市／敦煌書局全省連鎖門市

登記證／行政院新聞局局版臺業字第 288 號
印刷者／金濱印刷事業有限公司
初版／2014 年 8 月　定價／新台幣 399 元